ME, FRIDA,

and the Secret of the

PEACOCK

RING

ALSO BY ANGELA CERVANTES

Allie, First at Last

Gaby, Lost and Found

ME, FRIDA,

and the Secret of the

PEACOCK RING

ANGELA CERVANTES

Scholastic Press / New York

Library of Congress Cataloging-in-Publication Data available

ISBN 978-1-338-15931-8

10 9 8 7 6 5 4   19 20 21 22

Printed in the U.S.A.   23
First edition, April 2018

Book design by Nina Goffi

To Carlos, mi cielo

ME, FRIDA,

and the Secret of the

PEACOCK RING

Chapter 1

Adiós, Kansas

Whether she liked it or not, Paloma Marquez was in Mexico City for a whole month. She lifted her purple sleep mask and raised the plane's small window shade, letting a stream of sunlight pour in and light up the two books balanced on her lap. One was the newest book in her favorite mystery series featuring the superb teen sleuth Lulu Pennywhistle. Paloma finished it during the two-hour flight from Kansas City to Houston, where she and her mom made their connection flight to Mexico. Now Paloma had only the other book to entertain her during the rest of her time in Mexico. The small Spanish vocabulary book she had bought for the trip featured a yellow cartoon cat wearing a black Zorro mask and hat on the cover. Somewhere up in the sky between

Houston and Mexico City, she had opened it and studied a bunch of unfamiliar Spanish words until they blurred together like the passing clouds and put her to sleep like a Spanish lullaby.

"We're here!" her mom said. Seated next to her, she playfully tugged Paloma's arm. "Are you excited to be on your first trip out of the country? And in Mexico, no less! Did you ever think we would be traveling for the summer? Isn't it awesome?"

Paloma wasn't sure which question she should answer first, so she shut the window blind and tried out some Spanish. *"No quiero México. Tengo miedo de camarón."*

Her mother gave her a puzzled look. "I got the 'you don't want Mexico' part, but why are you scared of shrimp?"

Paloma frowned. "I meant 'change.' I don't like change."

"That would be *'cambio'* not *'camarón,'* but you get an A for effort." Her mom smiled. "C'mon, Paloma. Think of the adventure!"

"Aventura is overrated," Paloma answered. Her mom shook her head, and Paloma felt a shot of guilt straight through her heart.

Paloma wanted to be as pumped up as her mom was about this trip. She really did. After all, her mom had worked hard for this opportunity. It wasn't every day that a literature professor received a four-week fellowship to study abroad. For as long as Paloma could remember, her mom had been applying for fellowships in Mexico with no success. Still, after traveling almost seven hours to get to Mexico City, Paloma couldn't muster the energy for fake excitement. Did it make her a bad daughter to just want to spend a normal summer at home in Kansas reading her favorite mystery series at the pool and going to the mall with her friends Kate and Isha?

"Seriously, Paloma," her mom said. "You're the only one I know who complains about a free trip to Mexico." Her mom stood in the aisle to remove her backpack from the overhead compartment. "I thought that *at least* visiting your dad's old stomping grounds would fire you up."

She has a point, Paloma thought. But four weeks? Paloma's stomach twisted. She was losing most of her summer. What about the Fourth of July? Paloma, Kate, and Isha had been plotting a massive fireworks display at the lake. Every *boom, pop, pow* would be synchronized to their favorite songs, and they were going to come up with a sparkler routine. But because of this trip to Mexico, Paloma's summer plans had fizzled out.

The passengers began grabbing their bags and making their way into the aisle to exit the plane. Her mom stood aside to let Paloma slip ahead of her.

"Let's go, or as they say here in Mexico, *Vámonos.*"

Paloma tucked the books and eye mask into her bag and stepped off the plane with her mom into the crowded Jetway. She practiced a few Spanish phrases she thought would be useful during the four-week trip.

"No, gracias. No me gusta. No hablo español."

As she and her mom got into a long line behind the other passengers to show their passports, she continued. *"No quiero. No puedo. No me gusta."*

"Your Spanish sounds good, Paloma. You're a quick learner, but I think it's interesting that you've picked up all the negative expressions."

"I'm not negative." Paloma scowled.

"C'mon, Paloma. *'No me gusta.' 'No quiero.'* You don't like it. You don't want it. Tell me that's not all *negativo*." Her mom put her arm around Paloma's shoulders and gave her a squeeze. "I want you to have a positive experience here in Mexico. Try saying *'Me gusta'* instead."

Paloma let out a long sigh. "Fine. I don't know how to say 'I will try' in Spanish yet, but I will *try* to see this as one super-mega-positive experience that will forever change my life! I also want world peace, fluffy kittens, and unicorns!" Paloma forced a wide Miss America smile that showed all her teeth and lasted so long she felt like her cheeks would explode.

"Much better."

"Mom, why didn't you and Dad just raise me speaking Spanish? This whole trip would be so much easier, you know?" Paloma asked. "I mean, Dad was from Mexico, so he spoke Spanish like a pro, right? Did he ever try to teach me to speak it?"

"He did have a couple of cute Spanish nicknames for you," Paloma's mom said. A soft smile curved her lips as they took a few more steps in line. "Sometimes, he'd hold you and call you 'little bird' in Spanish. I don't remember the exact word anymore, but if I heard it, I'd know it."

"Lucky for you, I have a Spanish dictionary with a silly Zorro cat on the cover," Paloma quipped. "Surely *el gato* will know the answer." She opened the book and looked up the translation of "bird." Looking up the right word made Paloma feel like a detective searching for clues. But that was nothing new. She often hunted clues about her own life. Clues that proved, once upon a time, she had a dad.

A dad who was originally from Mexico. A dad whose name was Juan Carlos. A dad who studied architecture. A dad who her mom fell in love with at first sight when she met him at the university. A dad who stopped to help someone on the highway and never came home again.

Those were the cold, hard facts. Paloma had been only three years old when he died, and she depended on her mom to fill in the memory blanks. Luckily, her mom had plenty of memories to share: Halloween parties, college days, birthdays, Christmas . . . Every time her mom shared a memory, Paloma wrote it down on a note card and added it to her "memory box," a gift from her mom. It was just a regular craft box made of thick cardboard, no bigger than a pencil case. Paloma painted it purple and decorated it with butterflies. Along with the note cards, she filled it with photographs of her father and other small, sentimental trinkets. Separately, each item was a clue that told her something about her father.

Paloma hoped that if she could gather enough of them, she'd be able to finally understand the man he had been.

She always kept the box by her bedside, and sometimes before falling asleep, she'd stare at the photographs of her

handsome, dark-haired dad holding her in front of her birthday cake or pushing her in a stroller. She often hoped that if she stared long enough at a photograph, maybe the memory of that exact moment would rise up above all the others in her head the way their plane had risen high above the clouds. Then she'd have something real to hold. But it never happened. She always ended up right where she started, with no memories of her own. Perhaps she'd find a clue in Mexico that would finally reveal a real memory of her father that was all her own.

In the meantime, Paloma found the word she'd been looking for.

"*Pájaro,*" she said. "Is that the word he used to call me? Little bird?"

Her mom tilted her head. "Yes, that sounds about right."

Paloma pulled out a note card from her bag, wrote down "*pájaro.*" An immigration officer called them forward to review their passports. Her mom gave her a quick kiss on the forehead. "Let's go, my little bird."

When they had gotten through customs, Paloma studied the stamp on her passport: *Migración. La República de México.*

In the mystery books she read at home, Lulu Pennywhistle had already filled her passport with stamps from Dubai, London, and Berlin several times, but Paloma was pretty sure Lulu had never traveled to Mexico. Paloma liked that Mexico, the place where her dad was born, was her first out-of-the-USA trip. She glided her hand over the page with the fresh stamp.

"*Me gusta mucho,*" Paloma said quietly.

Chapter 2

A Hairy Four Weeks

"Mom, is someone picking us up?" Paloma asked. Her eyes darted over the crowd of people waiting for passengers outside the baggage claim area.

"The university is sending folks," her mom said, securing her backpack on her shoulder. "They said to meet near the exit, but is this the exit? Or do they mean outside?"

"How will we know who they are?" Paloma clutched her bag against her chest and followed her mom through the crowd. "What if we get into the wrong car and get kidnapped?"

"That's not going to happen."

"It could happen. Last night, Kate emailed me an article about all these kidnappings going on in Mexico."

"Such a nice friend," her mom said with a smirk.

"And Isha told me that there is this drug trafficking kingpin dude that will take us to a desert and demand ransom for us and—"

"No more nonsense, Paloma," her mom said in a stern voice. "Let's just wait over there by that little store."

As Paloma followed her mom, she scanned the crowd, looking for anyone holding a sign with her mom's name on it. But there were so many people. All of them hurried by, dragging luggage and speaking rapid-fire Spanish on cell phones. Paloma frowned. She felt stranded in a strange place.

"Maybe they forgot us. Can you call someone?" Paloma said just as a man walked by, slowing down to glance at Paloma and her mom. Paloma tugged on her mom's sleeve, but her mom was checking messages on her phone and didn't notice.

"Mom, there's a guy staring at—"

"Give me a minute, Paloma. The university left a voice mail."

The man looked back at Paloma before walking farther into the crowd. She felt her heart thump harder. Why had he looked back at her? Just like Lulu Pennywhistle, Paloma started making mental notes of the man's appearance in case she needed to report him to the police. He was medium height, had black hair and a brownish complexion, and wore khaki pants, tan loafers, a green polo shirt, and a brown leather messenger bag. Suddenly, he turned to look at Paloma once again, and their eyes met. Paloma turned away quickly, and found herself face-to-face with a large poster featuring a painting of a woman who had a faint mustache and thick dark eyebrows that stretched straight over her eyes and touched in the middle. Paloma thought it was called a unibrow.

"Whoa! Call the salon," she exclaimed. Paloma didn't know what was scarier: the man who kept staring at her or the woman in the poster. In it, a black cat lurked over the woman's left shoulder like it was ready to pounce. Over the other shoulder, a monkey picked at a necklace of tangled sticks that hung around the woman's neck. Dangling from the stick necklace was a black hummingbird. "Call animal control, too!"

"What, honey?" her mom asked. She took her eyes off her phone just long enough to see what Paloma was talking about. "Oh, it's a poster for Frida Kahlo's home! We're going to live nearby, I think."

"What do you mean?" Paloma glanced at the black cat and monkey in the painting. "At the circus?"

"Don't be silly," she answered, shaking her head. "It's an advertisement for the Frida Kahlo Museum in Coyoacán." She pointed at the words at the bottom of the poster.

La Casa Azul, Coyoacán, México

"Professor Emma Marquez?" said a man's voice from behind them. Paloma and her mom spun around. It was the man who had been staring at her. Paloma clutched her mom's arm.

"Yes, that's right," said Paloma's mom. "I'm Emma."

The man held out his hand. "I'm Professor Julian Breton from the university." Paloma's chest loosened. She was relieved he wasn't a kidnapper. "If you're ready, we can go. I hope you and your daughter weren't waiting too long."

"We just arrived and we're admiring the poster for Casa Azul," Paloma's mom said. "Is it close to the house we'll be staying in?"

"Your house is a few blocks from it. You'll be on Paris Street, and Casa Azul is on Londres Street. No more than a five-minute walk. We're going there tonight for an art reception."

"That's right," Paloma's mom gushed. "The reception is tonight! Thanks for the reminder. I'm looking forward to it."

"Mr. and Mrs. Farill will be there. They're eager to meet you."

"Who are they?" Paloma asked.

"The family that funded our trip here," Paloma's mom said. "They're wealthy patrons of the university. Is that right?" Paloma's mom looked over at Professor Breton for confirmation. He nodded and smiled. "Without their generosity, we'd be spending the summer back in Kansas City."

So they're to blame for dragging me away from my friends, Paloma thought. "Do I have to go?"

"Of course you're going," Paloma's mom said, narrowing her eyes at Paloma. "We'll get to see the home of the famous artist Frida Kahlo!"

"Do we have to wear our eyebrows like that?" Paloma said, pointing at the poster. "And I sort of left my bird necklaces at home. My bad."

Professor Breton laughed. "No bird necklace required."

"Don't be a goofball, Paloma," her mom said. "Frida was famous for her self-portraits. She once said she painted self-portraits because she knew herself best."

Paloma shrugged. "I know myself best, too, but I don't go around painting myself all day."

"Maybe you're not painting yourself, but I've seen you, Kate, and Isha run around taking selfies every second of the day, so don't be so quick to judge," her mom sassed back. "Plus, Frida Kahlo was one of your dad's favorite artists. Don't you want to find out why?"

Paloma gazed back at the poster. This woman with the black hummingbird necklace was one of her dad's favorite artists? Paloma pulled out a pen and note card and started writing.

"Is she still alive?" Paloma asked, copying Frida's name from the poster. "Does she still live in Mexico?"

"Frida died a long time ago, but her art is still highly revered in Mexico," Professor Breton said. "All around the world actually. I'm surprised you've never heard of her before."

"That's my fault," her mom said. "Paloma's father was from Mexico, but I haven't done a good job of exposing her to her Mexican heritage. That's why I brought her on this trip. I've enrolled her in your summer class, Introduction to Mexican Art and Culture." Paloma looked up from her note card. She didn't like to hear her mom mention the regrets she had about raising Paloma alone. Plus, Paloma was dreading summer school.

"I can't believe you've enrolled me in summer school," Paloma whined. "It's June, for summer's sake!"

"Don't worry, Paloma," Professor Breton said. "It's not as structured as regular school. We have fun. You'll enjoy it. And between my class and living in Coyoacán, you'll learn everything there is to know about Frida Kahlo."

Perfect, Paloma thought. If this unibrowed artist was the best thing Coyoacán had to offer, it was going to be a very hairy four weeks.

Chapter 3

Selfie Overload

Paloma lifted her suitcase onto the bed in her new room, which was painted a bright, cheerful yellow. She felt like a sunflower had swallowed her up, and she liked it. In Kansas, her walls were "barely beige." Paloma's mom had called it a "nice neutral color" that would match everything, but Paloma argued that "barely beige" was a crayon box reject and an insult to flowers and rainbows. At home, she covered the barely beige walls with as many posters as she could.

Paloma opened her suitcase and spread out jeans, T-shirts, sweaters, and a few colorful scarves. As much as she wanted to slip on her favorite comfy jeans, tonight's reception called for something a bit nicer, so she pulled out a black skirt and a cream-colored knit top. She had never been to a swanky reception where people drank wine and blabbered on about art. She'd only read about these kinds of parties in Lulu Pennywhistle novels. In one book, Lulu disguised herself as a coat-check assistant to spy on a prime suspect. She was clever like that, and of course, Lulu always caught the bad guy. If Paloma could find a mystery to investigate tonight, maybe the evening wouldn't be half bad.

An hour later, Professor Breton and her mom waited while Paloma finished pinning a purple flower, which she had picked from the garden, in her hair. They walked two blocks along Paris Street and took a left on Allende. They walked two more blocks, until they came upon a huge blue house.

"Whoa," Paloma said once they approached the corner of Allende and Londres. She gazed at the large blue house that covered almost an entire block. "It's. A. Bright. Blue. House."

"Welcome to Casa Azul. The home of Frida Kahlo and her husband, Diego Rivera!" Professor Breton exclaimed. "Two of Mexico's finest artists."

"Mom, can we paint our apartment blue when we get back home?" Paloma asked.

"I don't think our landlord would approve, sweetie," her mom answered.

"We should do it anyway," Paloma said.

Her mom shook her head, laughed, and put an arm around Paloma's shoulders.

Music poured from behind the walls of the museum. In

front, cars dropped off women draped in silk shawls, and men in dark suits. Paloma was admiring how fancy everyone looked when she noticed a woman seated on the sidewalk just a few steps away from the museum entrance. Spread out in front of her was a multicolored serape covered with jewelry. The woman looked about her mom's age. She wore her long dark hair piled on top of her head with a red headpiece and a flowing turquoise-blue wrap decorated with embroidered flowers. Large gold hoops dangled from her ears.

The woman called out to Paloma. "*Oye, jovencita*, I have beautiful rings and necklaces, charms to calm your spirit, and stones to read your future."

"How cool! It's a fortune-teller," Paloma's mom said. "Should we get our fortune read?" She nudged Paloma.

Paloma had only seen fortune-tellers at the Renaissance Festival. Her mom would pay twenty dollars to get her palm read, but Paloma always refused. "No way. I've read enough Lulu Pennywhistle books to know that fortune-tellers are always frauds," Paloma said, and hid herself behind her mom and Professor Breton. When she peeked out, the woman called out to her again.

"*Oye, mi reina!*"

"Not tonight, *gracias!*" Professor Breton waved at the woman, who nodded and busied herself with another couple. "That's peculiar," he said. "Usually the vendors hang out at the main plaza in the evening. She must have known there was going to be a big party here tonight."

Paloma followed Professor Breton and her mom into the museum but not without one last glimpse of the Fortune-Teller, who was suddenly on her cell phone.

"Who calls a fortune-teller?" she scoffed.

Once inside the museum, Professor Breton led them to a patio, also painted blue, and filled with large potted plants and trees decorated with silver metal stars that lit up. At the center of the patio, an all-female mariachi group performed a lively tune. Paloma had once seen a mariachi band play at a local Cinco de Mayo celebration, but the musicians had all been men dressed in black-and-silver suits. In this mariachi group, girls and women of all ages wore purple outfits, embellished with gold thread and buttons. The upbeat tempo of their music made Paloma want to dance, but she couldn't understand a word they sang.

Soon, Professor Breton was introducing Paloma and her mom to everyone he knew. After shaking hands with at least a dozen people Paloma couldn't communicate with, she couldn't take it anymore. She opened her small purse and grabbed her phone.

"Put that away, little bird," her mom said.

"But, Mom! I've got nothing to do here and no one to talk to," Paloma said, shoving the phone back into her purse. "There's no one my age here," she complained.

"Why don't you go and check out the mariachis," her mom said, and pointed. "Look, there's a young girl at the top of the steps with a trumpet. She's about to play something."

Paloma looked up and saw a girl with purple ribbons braided into her long dark hair. She held a shiny silver trumpet. The young mariachi winked down at a boy wearing a black knit hat, sitting on a bench below. The boy gave the young mariachi a thumbs-up. They had the same dark hair and looked to be the same age. Paloma wondered if they were brother and sister. How nice to have a brother, Paloma thought. If she had one, she wouldn't be so bored now.

Paloma sat down on a bench facing the balcony and watched as the mariachi girl tipped her trumpet to her lips and began a sweet, gentle melody. After she played a verse, another mariachi girl with a gold trumpet echoed the same verse from the garden. The slow, sad song captivated Paloma. She liked how after each verse, the two trumpet players moved through the crowd of guests, playing in different spots throughout the courtyard. To Paloma, it was if they were searching for each other.

If the song had lyrics to it, Paloma thought, the words would be about someone who was lost. Sort of how she felt in this strange place surrounded by fancy Spanish-speaking adults. Paloma had always wished she could be the kind of person who could walk into any room and start conversations with random people. Lulu Pennywhistle had the ability to chitchat with ease. This was what made her a superb detective. She'd enter any room and identify who she needed to meet, and in a flash she had folks laughing, offering to do favors for her, and inviting her to places like Aspen or Napa Valley.

Paloma looked back at her mom. She, along with all of the other party guests, watched the trumpet players as they played side by side now. Their silky melody covered the cool night like a much-needed poncho. Aside from this bright blue house, these mariachi girls were the coolest things Paloma had seen in Mexico so far.

That is, until she saw a tall, slender boy with light brown hair and blue eyes who stood on the other side of the patio. He wore a sky-blue polo shirt with beige pants and loafers. Paloma met his eyes, and he waved at her. She looked behind her. When she saw no one else, she turned back to catch him point at her as if to say, "I'm waving at you." Paloma felt her whole face warm. When the song was done, everyone applauded, and the boy crossed the patio toward her.

Paloma sat up straight and touched the purple flower in her hair to make sure it was still there.

"Hola. Soy Tavo," the boy said, extending his hand to her. Up close, he was the cutest boy she'd ever seen. Paloma tried to ignore his blue eyes and focus instead on how she should answer in Spanish. It seemed to her like an eternity before she finally mustered the words.

"No hablo español," she said, standing to shake his hand.

"You're from the United States, aren't you?" the boy said, switching to English, with a sparkle in his blue eyes.

Paloma nodded and smiled, relieved that he spoke English.

"I knew it! I go to school in Arizona, but I spend my summers here or in Barcelona. What's your name?"

"Paloma," she said. "I'm from Kansas."

Tavo raised his eyebrows in disbelief. "What are you doing here?"

"It's my mom's fault. She was invited to study at the university for four weeks."

"Four weeks? That's enough time," he said, folding his arms against his chest.

Paloma shook her head. "What do you mean? Enough time for what? To learn Spanish?"

"For me to get to know you."

"Oh . . ." Paloma said, and readjusted the flower in her hair. She wasn't sure what else to say. No boy had ever just come out and said he wanted to get to know her before. "So what grade are you in?"

"Seventh grade," he said quickly. "Junior high. How about you?"

"Me too."

He stopped a waiter, grabbed two cups of punch, and handed one to Paloma. She sipped the frosty white drink, liking it immediately.

"What is this yummy stuff?" She chugged the punch.

"*Guanábana*. You like it?"

"Like it? I want to grow up and marry it. What kind of

fruit is it? And why don't they sell *gua-nah-ba-nah* in Kansas? It's so good."

Tavo chuckled at her exaggerated pronunciation. "So . . . you like Coyoacán so far?"

Paloma wrinkled her eyebrows. "I like the punch."

"That's it?" Tavo frowned.

Paloma bit down on her bottom lip. She hoped she hadn't offended him. "Sorry, it's just my first day here and so far— I'm super bored. I don't speak Spanish and I'm not really into art. But that last song with the trumpets was cool."

Tavo nodded. "Yeah, the song is called '*El niño perdido.*'" Paloma nodded but didn't know what it meant. "'The Lost Boy,'" Tavo added.

Paloma took a step back, shocked that she had somehow known the song had something to do with being lost. Was she turning mega intuitive like Lulu Pennywhistle?

"It was so sweet at the end when the trumpet players find each other like a lost child finding his mom," she said.

"Or a lonely boy like me finding a bored girl like you." Tavo smiled, causing Paloma's heart to somersault. *Is he really lonely? Not possible! He's too cute to be lonely.*

"Before your head blows up from boredom, can I show you something inside the museum?" Paloma nodded, and he led her across the patio toward the museum.

Her mom, who was laughing with Professor Breton and an elegant couple Paloma hadn't met yet, shot her a look of concern. Paloma pulled Tavo back to make introductions.

"Mom, this is Tavo. He's going to show me the house."

"Nice to meet you, Tavo. Your parents were just telling me about you," she said, giving a sideways glance to the elegant couple next to her. Paloma saw the resemblance right away. The man shared Tavo's blondish-brown hair, blue eyes, and chiseled chin. "Mr. and Mrs. Farill, this is my daughter, Paloma."

"Hi," Paloma said. "Wow, you look like a supermodel!" Paloma gushed at Tavo's mom.

"She's a former Miss Barcelona." Mr. Farill beamed and gave his wife a gentle kiss on her cheek.

"So cool," Paloma said.

Suddenly, Tavo slapped a hand over his forehead. "Wait a minute! That means that you're the American professor studying here with the university program my dad funds."

"That's me! The one and only!" Paloma's mom exclaimed. Paloma rolled her eyes. "Thanks to your parents' generosity, I'll be studying Mexican literature for four weeks."

Tavo winced. "Yikes! I'd die of boredom. Are you sure you should be thanking them?"

Paloma's mom laughed along with the Farills, which Paloma found annoying because whenever she told her mom something was boring, her mom gave her a stern lecture full of professor talk.

"No thanks required," Mr. Farill jumped in. "I'm happy to support cultural and educational exchanges."

Tavo faked an exaggerated yawn, making Paloma giggle.

"Anyway, I'd like to show Paloma a painting inside Frida's house. Is that okay?"

"Fine by me!" Paloma's mom smiled and shrugged. "I'm glad she's met someone her age."

As Tavo and Paloma walked away, Paloma heard her mom laugh again. It had been a while since she heard her mom laugh so much. At home, her mom threw herself into her work and rarely went out unless it was to a work event. Hearing her mom so happy made Paloma smile.

She followed Tavo up the stairs in the museum toward Frida's studio. As soon as they entered the studio, Paloma saw the mariachi girl who played the silver trumpet and the boy in the black hat standing next to each other by a window that looked out on the patio below. They whispered back and forth to each other in Spanish, and didn't notice Paloma and Tavo enter the room. When they finally realized they weren't alone anymore, they exchanged a panicked look. Paloma wondered what they had been discussing, but Tavo took no notice of them.

"So, since our parents know each other and we'll be hanging out a lot together these next four weeks, you should know one of my favorite painters," Tavo announced, and then pointed to a painting that hung on a wall. "This is Frida Kahlo. She was the queen of the selfies."

Once again, Paloma was face-to-face with another self-portrait of the artist. It was similar to the poster Paloma had seen earlier at the airport, except there was no cat and monkey lurking over her shoulders nor a black humming-bird dangling from her neck. In this painting, Frida wore a brown shawl and had a necklace of thorns piercing her skin. At the bottom of the painting was a message in Spanish.

"I saw another selfie of hers at the airport," Paloma said. "I thought it was a promotion for a circus, because it had a monkey in it."

Tavo chuckled. From the corner of her eye, Paloma glanced toward the window. The mariachi girl cradled her trumpet and wiped it with a cloth, while the boy watched someone or something below on the patio. Paloma thought he was as cute as Tavo but in a different way. Besides the black knit hat, he wore a dozen leather straps around his wrist and a couple of long leather cords with silver medallions around his neck. Sketching pencils and thin paintbrushes stuck out of his back jean pockets. Was he an artist like Frida?

Paloma watched as the boy nudged the mariachi girl, pointed at something down below, and then whispered in her ear. The girl scowled. When the boy caught Paloma's glance, he smiled at her. Paloma's heart pounded fast. She wanted to tell them how much she liked the mariachi song with the two trumpets, but she didn't know the words in Spanish and wasn't sure they spoke or understood English.

"Earlier, you said you were bored. I know what you mean," Tavo said, snapping Paloma's attention back to the painting. "Some art can be seriously dull, but there is nothing boring about Frida. She painted really amazing, sometimes gross paintings with blood and people jumping off buildings, but that's what I like about her work. She's not hiding the truth about life." Tavo turned around and gestured toward a metal wheelchair behind them. It was positioned in front of an easel holding a painting of watermelons. "Like, for example, Frida almost died when she was eighteen years old."

"What happened to her?"

"She was in a bus accident coming home from school. After the accident, she was stuck in bed, and that's when she began to paint."

Paloma looked over at the wheelchair and then back to the self-portrait. She wished she could say something super smart to impress Tavo, but the mention of a bus accident that almost killed Frida stuck in her head. She thought about her own dad stopping on the highway to help an elderly couple. It was winter. The roads were icy. Her father had just helped the couple, when another car struck him. If her father had survived, would he have needed a wheelchair or crutches for the rest of his life like Frida? Paloma shuddered, her eyes brimming with tears. She needed a distraction, so she gazed at the painting of watermelons positioned on the easel. On one of the watermelons were the words *"viva la vida."*

"'Viva la vida'?" Paloma asked, tapping Tavo's arm. "What does it mean?"

"'Long live life,'" he said. "This is one of Frida's last paintings before she died."

"Viva la vida," Paloma repeated. Something about those

words warmed her all over. It made the sadness she felt vanish as quickly as it had appeared. She turned back to the self-portrait and narrowed in on Frida Kahlo's serious brown eyes. Those eyes didn't show a woman in pain.

To Paloma, her expression was one of strength. And yet . . . a thorn necklace pierced the artist's neck, drawing specks of blood. Dangling from one ear was a hand-shaped earring. Behind her were dark olive-green leaves and what looked like the Kansas sky when it was about to thunderstorm: hints of pale pink, smoky white, and gray.

"But why all these thorns, the message in Spanish, and the thick hairy eyebrows?" Paloma said. "Didn't they make tweezers when she was alive?"

The mariachi girl suddenly giggled, and Paloma looked back at her. Did she understand English? But before Paloma could ask, the girl said something in Spanish to the boy, then turned back toward the window. Paloma felt so stupid. She was surrounded by people she couldn't understand and art that was even more mind-boggling.

"Everyone has their own ideas about Frida's paintings," Tavo said. "I know she was definitely trying to tell us something, but sometimes I'm not so sure what that was."

Again, Paloma focused on Frida's eyes. The eyebrows no longer looked overgrown or hairy. Instead, they looked like the perfect wings of a bird taking flight. Did Frida want to fly away?

"Have you ever heard of the Lulu Pennywhistle mystery books?"

"Mysteries aren't my thing," Tavo said with a shrug.

"Well, Lulu is really cool. She solves these impossible cases with just a few clues. It's sort of like interpreting a painting," Paloma said. "The artist has given us clues. We have to figure it out. A thorn necklace isn't just a thorn necklace. It means something. I'm just not sure exactly what because I don't know enough about her yet."

Tavo raised his eyebrows and made an explosion noise. "You just blew my mind."

Paloma chuckled. "Whatever. Don't get too excited. I'm not good at art stuff, but I do like mysteries."

Paloma heard the two kids whispering, and glanced toward the window. Whatever they had been watching outside on the patio no longer interested them. Their eyes were glued to Paloma. She now knew that they must understand every single word she said. After all, the mariachi girl had laughed when Paloma mentioned the tweezers. Plus, they were leaning in the way Paloma and Isha did at school when they eavesdropped on teachers in the lunchroom. Why were they suddenly so interested in what she had to say? She tried to refocus on the painting.

"I'm not totally sure . . ." Paloma started, "but I feel like she's telling us not to be fake in our lives."

Suddenly, the boy grabbed the mariachi girl's hand, and

they rushed out of the studio. Tavo spun around and watched them leave as if just noticing them for the first time.

"They were in a hurry," he said.

Paloma frowned. She lost her chance to tell the mariachi girl that she loved that song. What was it called? *"El niño perdido"*?

Tavo turned back to Paloma. "And you have the nerve to say you're not good at this art stuff."

Paloma shrugged. "With you, art doesn't seem so boring." Silently, she added that with him around, Mexico for four weeks didn't seem so boring, either.

Chapter 4

Tell No One

Paloma leaned against her mom and gazed over the museum's courtyard, and the exotic plants and sculptures that filled it. Waiters collected wineglasses as the mariachis packed up their instruments. A few guests remained chatting in the courtyard, saying their good-byes. Ever since Tavo had left with his parents an hour ago, Paloma couldn't stop yawning. Before leaving, his parents had invited Paloma and her mom over to their home for dinner. Paloma couldn't wait to see Tavo again. She decided that her first day in Coyoacán wasn't as horrible as she had thought it would be. Paloma had worn a purple flower in her hair, met a cute boy, learned about Frida Kahlo, and listened to mariachi music. Now she was exhausted.

"Just think, Paloma, Frida Kahlo used to hold amazing parties with famous actors, musicians, and artists in this very spot," said Paloma's mom, putting her arm around her shoulders. "Isn't that fascinating?"

"If you say so," Paloma said, yawning and rubbing her tired eyes. When she opened them back up, the mariachi girl and the boy in the black hat were suddenly standing in front of her.

"Paloma, did you meet Gael and Lizzie Castillo?" Paloma's mom asked.

Lizzie smiled and stepped forward to plant a kiss on Paloma's cheek. "Welcome to Mexico," she said with a slight accent. Gael leaned forward and gave her a peck on the cheek, too. Paloma couldn't help but jerk backward in surprise. In Kansas, boys didn't kiss girls on the cheek when they met. Especially boys with adorable dimples.

"Gael and Lizzie speak perfect English and are about your age. Twelve, right?"

"Yes," answered Gael. "Lizzie is my big sister by twenty minutes, so she thinks that makes her my boss." Gael nudged Lizzie playfully, and she rolled her eyes.

"Do you have any annoying little brothers or sisters?" Lizzie asked.

"No, it's just me. Me and my mom," Paloma said, and her mom kissed the top of her head. "Mom," Paloma complained. Lizzie and Gael smiled.

"Sorry, little bird. Anyway, Lizzie and Gael are part of the university's language program. They'll be your tutors to help you with your Spanish. Isn't that cool?"

Paloma nodded. "Thanks. I'll need all the help I can get."

"In return, you can help them with their English. Although their English is very good, they both want to improve their informal dialogue."

"Informal what? Stop talking like a professor, Mom," Paloma said.

"Casual conversation, chitchat, you know?" Paloma's mom explained.

"I have to practice my English because someday I'll go to New York for my own art exhibit. You and I can have an *intercambio*. I don't know that word in English," Gael said.

"That's okay. I don't know it, either, but I get what you mean." Paloma laughed and turned to Lizzie.

"That song you played . . . with the other trumpet player?" Paloma said. "It was so amazing. I really liked—" Paloma tried to suppress a yawn, but it came out as embarrassing yawn-talk. Paloma winced. "Sorry."

"It's okay," Lizzie said. "I'm super tired, too."

"Ready to go?" Paloma's mom patted her head. Paloma nodded, and her mom glanced at her hair. "Your flower blew away."

Paloma reached for the top of her head. "Oh no! I loved that flower. I wanted to keep it to remember my first night here." Then she saw it near a large potted plant. She and Gael rushed for it, but he reached it first and held it out to her.

"Your memory is saved," he said.

"Thanks." Paloma smiled and took it from him, but he handed her more than the flower. A small folded note pricked her fingers.

"*Hasta luego*, Paloma," he said, and walked away with Lizzie before she had a chance to ask him about it. She glanced at the folded note and slid it into her purse along with the purple flower.

Paloma set a fast pace for the walk back to the rented house. Her mom kept complaining about her feet, but Paloma had to get back so she could read the note in private. What was it about?

As soon as she got home, Paloma kicked off her shoes and headed to her room. She lay down on the bed and unfolded the note. On the front of the note was a sketch of an eye. *That's weird,* she thought. The note read:

Dear Paloma,

A great injustice has happened at Casa Azul. Frida Kahlo and the people of Mexico need your help to solve a mystery and make things right! Can you help us? Tell no one you received this note. It's a matter of life and death. We'll be in contact.

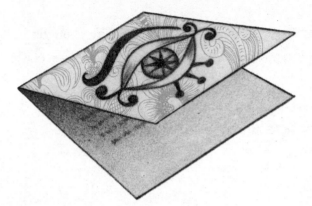

Was this some sort of joke? Paloma chewed on her thumbnail and considered her options. Should she tell her mom? Show her the note? But the note said, "Tell no one. It's a matter of life and death." Whose life? Whose death? Paloma read the note again, and stopped on the last line. "We'll be in contact."

Who is "we"? Did Gael and Lizzie belong to some secret organization? And why did they think she could help them?

At times like these, spunky teen detective Lulu Pennywhistle would cross her arms and say, "What mighty high jinks is this?" and rush off to solve the mystery of the day. But Paloma was no Lulu.

"No puedo," Paloma said. "No way."

She opened her memory box and tossed the wilting purple flower atop the note cards and photographs of her dad.

Lulu Pennywhistle never turned down anyone in need of help. Especially "life-and-death" help. But Paloma knew that real life was more complicated. She thought of her dad, and reminded herself that helping people could be dangerous.

"I'll leave the mysteries to Lulu," she said out loud, and threw the note into the wastebasket.

Chapter 5

Mighty High Jinks

In front of the Casa Azul museum, Paloma walked toward the Fortune-Teller.

"Come sit down. Let's chitchat," the Fortune-Teller said, waving Paloma closer. Paloma sat across from her. Beautiful silver earrings shaped like birds and beaded necklaces with large stones were laid out on the blanket between them. Paloma wanted to touch each one because they were like no jewelry she'd ever seen. Every stone glowed. Every gem sparkled. Each piece of silver shined. When the woman raised her head, it wasn't the Fortune-Teller. Instead, it was the woman from the paintings. It was Frida Kahlo.

"It's you," Paloma whispered. "How?"

"I wanted to talk *un poco* with you because you're an interesting girl," Frida said, picking up a jade ring from her blanket, inspecting it, and putting it back down. She wore a red blouse and long floral skirt, a headdress of yellow and orange flowers, and a chunky necklace of coral stones. A pair of small hand-shaped earrings dangled from her ears. Paloma knew she had seen those earrings somewhere before, but where?

"Am I dreaming?" Paloma asked. Frida picked up a red oval stone, studied it, and put it back down.

"*Sí,*" Frida said as her bright eyes locked with Paloma's sleepy brown ones. She picked up a pair of dangling turquoise earrings to inspect.

Paloma gazed downward to a smooth black hummingbird necklace. She couldn't help but want to glide her hand over it. "You have so many pretty things. Are you looking for something to wear?" Paloma asked as Frida put down the turquoise earrings and then selected a long string of beads. "Can I help you find something?"

"What is lost is lost," Frida answered with a slight shrug and soft smile.

Paloma shook her head. "What do you mean? What have you lost?"

"It's true I am missing something . . ." she said, securing a sky-blue shawl over her shoulders. "But you're missing something, too, Paloma." Frida gazed warmly at her. "I hope you'll find it in my beautiful *ciudad*."

*   *   *

"*My beautiful* ciudad. *My beautiful city,*" Paloma mumbled, waking up slowly.

She peeked from under her purple eye mask to confirm she was not outside having a bizarre sidewalk chat with the deceased Mexican artist but inside her bright yellow room. She glanced at the clock, threw the comforter off her bed, got up, and snatched the note from the wastebasket.

Frida was a dream. The note was not.

Her bedroom door creaked open and her mom poked her head inside the room. "Good, you're up! We have guests. They brought us some—"

"Guests? Is it Tavo?"

"No, it's Gael and Lizzie. They're here to practice *español* with you. Which is *muy* cool." Paloma's mom beamed.

Paloma narrowed her eyes.

"How did they know where we live?" Paloma asked, pulling a purple hoodie over her pajamas. "Isn't that strange to you?"

"Not strange at all. After they told me they were part of Professor Breton's language program, I gave them our address so they could come over and start the *intercambio* with you. I didn't really expect them to come so soon, but I like their dedication. Maybe it will rub off on you."

Paloma frowned. Dedicated or not, she didn't trust anyone who showed up at her house before nine in the morning, and she certainly didn't trust anyone who passed her a note about a so-called "mystery." What sort of mighty high jinks was this?

"They brought us Mexican pastries. So hurry up and get out here. It's rude to keep friends waiting."

Paloma clenched the note in her fist.

"Friends? I just met them last night," Paloma blurted.

Her mom shut the door behind her and folded her arms across her chest.

"You seemed fine with this last night. Why the sudden attitude? They're nice kids who are going to help you with your Spanish," her mom said.

The note was burning a hole in Paloma's hand. Would "nice kids" pass her a weird note about "life and death" and warn her to "tell no one"? She didn't think so! Paloma lifted the note up but then thought against it. Showing her mom the mysterious note was totally against Lulu Pennywhistle code. Lulu never shared a case with an adult *unless* it was a total last resort. Paloma lowered her hand.

"It's just that I barely know them," Paloma said.

"You're in Mexico. You don't know anyone here. This is your chance to make friends and learn Spanish." Her mom shrugged. "Think about it. You have a rare opportunity in front of you. You get to learn how Mexicans really speak, not just what they teach you in the classroom. It'll be fun!"

"Fun? That's not fun," Paloma whined. "That's like those

mini 'fun-size' candy bars. There is nothing fun about small candy. And I promise you, there's nothing fun about learning a language."

Her mom raised her eyebrows. "Your dad spoke fluent Spanish and English. You're his daughter. If he could do it, you can."

Paloma knew she was beat. She tightened her fist around the note. "Okay. I'll practice Spanish with them."

"Good. Get dressed and get out here." Her mom left, closing the door behind her.

"Fun-size candy?" Paloma grumbled as she tossed the wadded note onto her vanity. "Really, Paloma? Is that all you could come up with?" She frowned at herself in the mirror and ran a comb through her straight brown hair. She pinned a few strands back from her face. "Lulu would have had a better comeback than that."

In the face of danger, Lulu Pennywhistle always searched for the positive. Paloma began to consider that Gael's visit was a good thing. Now she could question him. *He can't just hand a girl a note about a "great injustice" and expect her to drop everything to help him,* Paloma thought.

She put the note inside her hoodie pocket along with a few note cards and joined them at the kitchen table.

Gael was deep into a story. "So then my dad, being a great artist, told the New York people that there was no way he could—"

Seeing Paloma, Gael stopped midsentence. He and Lizzie stood up and gave Paloma a kiss on the cheek. "*Buenos días, Paloma!*" Gael said. "Now you try it."

Paloma stood frozen. "Try what?" She looked at her mom for help. Her mom mouthed the words to her. "Oh! *Buenos días*," Paloma said, and sat down. Gael and Lizzie clapped.

"You'll be a Spanish speaker in no time!" Gael said with a wink. Paloma eyed him suspiciously.

"Well, I hope I get the chance to meet your father someday," Paloma's mom said. "I really have a deep respect for all artists."

"He'll be back in a few weeks," Gael said. "It's only a short trip."

Paloma caught Lizzie shooting a strange look at Gael. Paloma wasn't sure how to interpret it. She watched Gael closely, but he seemed oblivious to her gaze. In between bites of pastry and sips of juice, he continued his story about his dad's travel to New York. His English had a slight touch of an accent that most girls would find super cute, but Paloma had read enough mystery books to know not to be fooled by dimples and an adorable accent.

"How did you learn to speak English so well?" Paloma asked.

"You think my English is good? Thanks for that. Seriously, that makes my day," Gael gushed.

Paloma gave him a puzzled look, but he didn't answer her question.

Lizzie cleared her throat. "Our mom was an English teacher," she explained, shaking her head at her brother. "We speak it at home."

"And we listen to a lot of music and watch all the Hollywood movies," Gael added.

Gael started singing a song in English that Paloma had heard a few times on the radio. Her mom quickly joined him in singing the chorus. Paloma sunk down in her chair in embarrassment. As Gael sang across the table from her, she made mental notes about him. Under his black knit hat, he had dark, chin-length hair and light brown eyes. He wore jeans, a long-sleeved T-shirt, and the same two silver medallions he'd worn at the party the night before. They must be special if he wore them every day.

Once Gael was done singing, he talked nonstop about his dad's work. He paused every once in a while when he struggled with an English word. At that point, Lizzie would jump in with the correct translation. Other than that, she was mostly quiet.

Paloma turned her attention to Lizzie, who was dressed in a red plaid shirt over black leggings, and black flats. Her dark brown hair was pulled into a neat bun, and she wore a small gold crucifix around her neck. Paloma decided that Lizzie was probably the more sensible of the two Castillos. It certainly wasn't Gael. No sensible person would ask a total stranger for help by slipping them a secret note.

Finally, Paloma could no longer stand the breakfast table chitchat. It was time to get answers.

"I'm ready to practice some serious *español* now!" Paloma said, interrupting Gael.

"You are?" her mom asked.

"Yep! Let's get to it." Paloma stood up and slid her chair back. "I've only got four weeks to learn this language." Paloma marched outside to the patio. Gael and Lizzie excused themselves and followed after her.

Outside, Gael pulled note cards from his back pocket. They were the same type of note cards that Paloma used to write down her memories.

"What are those for?" she asked him. "I have note cards just like that."

"We can use them to write down new vocabulary," Gael answered. "What do you use your note cards for?"

Paloma fingered the note cards in her hoodie pocket that she always kept nearby in case her mom shared a memory, but she wasn't going to tell him about them. It was none of his business. She looked back toward the breakfast table inside, ignoring his question. Her mom was tidying up and out of earshot.

"Okay, drop the charade," Paloma threatened in her best Lulu Pennywhistle impression. "I know you're not here to practice Spanish with me. I read the note."

"Yes, the note . . ." Gael trailed off.

"Did you know that your brother passed me a cray-cray note about a life-and-death mystery?" Paloma asked Lizzie, extending the wrinkled note to her.

Lizzie stepped back with a look of confusion. "Cray cray?" she asked, taking the note from Paloma. "Is that even English?"

Gael pulled out a pen.

"Is that a 'c' or 'k'?" he asked as he started to write the term on one of his note cards.

"Doesn't matter," Paloma said, and rolled her eyes. "Anyway, it means 'crazy.' It was a crazy note about a great injustice at Casa Azul." Lizzie read the note and then handed it to Gael, who had an amused look on his face. "And here's another way to use it. Last night, I had a cray-cray dream about Frida Kahlo because of that note." She turned back to Lizzie. "So did you know, or didn't you?"

"Yes, I told him it was, as you say, cray cray to involve you because you're not from here, but he insisted that you be the one to help us," Lizzie said. "*Personalmente*, I don't think you have the *valor* to help us."

"What? What is that? *Valor?*"

"Courage," Gael said. "Here's a note card if you want to write it down." He held out his pen and a blank note card. Paloma frowned, waved it away, and pulled out her own note card from her pocket and jotted it down.

"I'm brave," she said. "I have *valor*. I came to Mexico, didn't I?"

43

Gael nodded. "Yes, that's super brave." Paloma couldn't tell if Gael was making fun of her. Lizzie rolled her eyes.

"I told you, we shouldn't have involved her," Lizzie said. "She's not from here. She is used to the simple life on a Kansas farm, not helping to solve a major mystery."

"Hey!" Paloma protested. "I don't live on a farm. I live in an apartment near a huge mall with a big food court that has pizza, sushi, and a Panda Express restaurant."

"Superman was raised on a farm in Kansas, Lizzie," Gael said in a soothing voice. "He is the most brave. She can help us." Gael gave his sister a pleading look.

Paloma grabbed her head in frustration. "For the last time, I don't live on a farm. And guess what. I'll be the one deciding whether I want to be involved." Paloma crossed her arms. "Now, what is this whole so-called injustice about?"

Gael pulled out a chair from the patio table for Paloma. "I will explain everything, but you should sit."

Chapter 6

The Tale of the Missing Peacock Ring

"The mystery begins in 1954," Gael started. "The year Frida Kahlo died."

Paloma sat next to him at the patio table with the soft lime-green cushions and tablecloth. Lizzie, looking very annoyed, sat across from her. "But for us, the mystery began two weeks ago when our dad left for New York City."

"Before he left, we overheard our dad talking to a friend on the phone about a peacock ring that the brilliant artist Frida Kahlo designed. She loved peacocks and wanted it as a birthday gift to herself."

"She was very ill at the time," Lizzie added. Paloma thought about the wheelchair she'd seen in Frida's studio the night before. "She was stuck in bed all day. Frida knew she had only a few more days of life left," Lizzie continued. Her voice was filled with such sudden sadness that Paloma got goose bumps.

"Her husband, the artist Diego Rivera, gave her the stones and helped her make the ring since she was so sick, but then she died and the ring disappeared."

"Disappeared? How?" Paloma asked.

"That's the mystery. No one knows. When Frida died, Diego was devastated. He said it was like the worst, most tragic day of his life. He locked up some of her jewelry and clothes in a room at Casa Azul and refused to let anyone inside."

"Why?"

"*No sé.* I don't know. Before Diego died, he asked a close friend named Dolores to make sure the room remained locked. It stayed that way until she died in 2002. A couple of years later, they found a note from Dolores that revealed the location of the locked room. At that point, the museum opened it."

Paloma did the math in her head and gasped. "That's, like, fifty years! I don't get it. What was Diego scared of so much that he'd want to keep Frida's jewelry locked up for so long?"

"Good question," Gael said.

"Maybe to protect it and preserve it for the people of Mexico?" Lizzie said. "Frida was *muy mexicana.*"

"Muy mexicana," Paloma repeated, liking how it sounded. She wrote it down on a note card.

"Diego made a list of everything that was locked inside the room. The peacock ring was supposed to be there, but when they opened it, it wasn't."

Gael passed Paloma a note card. "Here, I sketched it. The peacock ring was especially valuable because Frida had designed it herself. When Diego had it made, he used real emeralds that supposedly belonged to Cuauhtémoc, the last Aztec king, and blue sapphires worn by Cuauhtémoc's daughters. The silver was from the mines of Taxco."

Paloma gazed over his sketch. She had to admit, he had some mad drawing skills. If the ring was truly made from emerald and sapphire, it was probably worth millions. "This is cool, but doesn't exactly sound life-and-death, you know?"

"But it is a great injustice, no?" Gael said. "If we find this ring for Frida and for Mexico, we'll receive a reward! And you will be famous in Mexico, Paloma. Especially if we find it before Frida's birthday on July 6. There's going to be a big party at Casa Azul, and we could show everyone that we found the ring. That would be cray cray, right?"

"Okay, stop using 'cray cray' right now. I'm sorry I ever taught you that word," Paloma snapped. She gazed over the peacock ring sketch. July 6 was a couple of weeks away. It wasn't a lot of time. "So you want to find this ring just to get a big reward?"

"A huge reward. Cool, right?" Gael nodded.

Paloma frowned. Lulu Pennywhistle didn't take cases to win rewards. She craved justice. Not the spotlight. Not money.

"Actually, we want to find it because it belongs at Casa Azul," Lizzie said, sensing Paloma's hesitation. "She designed it. It should be on display at the museum like the rest of her art."

Paloma nodded. Now, that was a Lulu Pennywhistle–worthy reason. But how could she help them? She didn't speak Spanish. She knew nothing about art or Frida Kahlo. Paloma frowned and shook her head.

"See, she's not interested in helping us. I told you, *hermano*," Lizzie said, leaning back in her chair. "She's just like her name. A little pigeon who drops by to get a few fun scraps and then flies off back to Kansas and her huge mall."

"What do you mean like my name?"

Gael laughed nervously. "She just means that your name

in *español* is how we call the cray-cray birds that eat scraps in the plaza."

Paloma scowled. Not only was Gael still using "cray cray," but now Lizzie was comparing her to a filthy pigeon.

She had always been told that her name meant "dove." Doves represented peace and love. At a cousin's wedding, the bride and groom had released white doves at the end of the ceremony. That was the kind of "Paloma" she was. Peaceful. Loving. Not a gross pigeon. Had her mom been wrong about the correct translation of her name for all these years?

"Look, I'm not from here," Paloma said. As soon as she released those words, she felt a pang of guilt. Her father was from Mexico. If he's from Mexico . . . wasn't she, in a round-about way, also from Mexico? Paloma pushed away from the patio table. "And my mom has enrolled me in summer school. I don't have a lot of free time. Sorry."

Gael winced.

"We don't need your help anyway, Kansas," Lizzie said, grabbing her bag from the table. She stomped out of the patio and back into the house. Paloma could see her just inside the door, waiting for Gael. He gathered his note cards and stood up to leave, but hesitated.

"If you change your mind, you can find us near my aunt's churros stand by the coyote fountain," he said.

"I'm not going to change my mind."

Gael gave Paloma a faint smile and stepped closer to her. "Do you want to know why I thought you could help us?"

Paloma looked down at her flip-flops to avoid his soft, sad brown eyes.

"It's because that night at the reception, you were wearing a purple flower in your hair. I thought to myself, that is something very Frida."

Paloma gazed up at him. Why was he making her feel bad about this? They barely knew each other.

"Then later I heard you say to Tavo Farill that you thought Frida was trying to tell us 'not to be fake' in our lives. I believe that, too."

Gael leaned in and gave her a quick kiss on the cheek. "*Nos vemos*, Paloma."

Chapter 7

Courage

From the living room window, Paloma watched Gael and Lizzie walk out the front gate.

"What the heck does '*nos vemos*' mean?" Paloma asked out loud.

"What, honey?" her mom asked from the computer desk.

"'*Nos vemos*'? What does that mean?"

"'See you around,'" Paloma's mom answered. "Everything go okay? Gael and Lizzie didn't stay very long."

"They taught me how to say 'courage' in Spanish, and I taught them 'cray cray.'"

"Why did you teach them . . . Never mind. I guess it's a start, but I wish . . ." her mom began, and then let the rest of her thought fade.

"What do you wish?" Paloma turned away from the window and walked over to see what her mom was doing at the computer. The screen showed a picture of Paloma's dad in Teotihuacán, Mexico, sitting atop the sun pyramid. Blue sky and fluffy white clouds hovered around him. Her mom clicked a button, and the printer hummed to life. As the picture came out, Paloma wished that memories of her father were as easily produced.

"I was hoping you would embrace this opportunity more seriously," her mom finally said.

"Mom, it's summer vacation. I'm supposed to be at the pool with my friends. Not here embracing serious opportunities."

"Okay, Paloma." Her mom raised her hands in surrender. "I just hoped you'd enjoy being in a new place, making new friends and learning Spanish."

"Oh yeah, speaking of Spanish. Was it Dad's or your idea to name me after a filthy pigeon?"

Her mom chuckled. Paloma didn't think it was funny at all.

"What are you talking about? We named you after a dove."

"Which also happens to be the same word for 'pigeon.' Gael and Lizzie also taught me that. It was a very eye-opening *intercambio*. Thank you very much," Paloma said.

Her mom shook her head. "No, we named you after a sweet little dove. Hand me that silver frame."

Paloma scanned the room, found the empty frame on a bookshelf, and handed it to her mom. She sat down on the couch.

"What are you doing?"

"I woke up this morning and looked around and thought it'd be nice to have some pictures of your dad here. He had always planned to bring us to Mexico. He wanted to take you when you were old enough to appreciate things, but . . ." Her mom's voice trailed off.

Paloma was used to this. She knew the ending of that sentence. She'd heard it many times. Where did the rest of those words go? It was another mystery.

Her mom put the picture into the frame and placed it next to a vase of calla lilies on the top of the bookshelf. "Being in Mexico, even for just the one day we've been here, is triggering memories. I'm remembering things about your dad that I haven't thought about in years." She pulled off her wedding ring and handed it to Paloma. "Like my wedding ring. Your grandma gave it to your dad before she died. It's red opal from Mexico."

"Dad's mom? Did you ever meet her?"

Her mom shook her head. "No. Your dad's parents passed away before we met."

Paloma felt the cool smoothness of the red stone. She had touched this ring many times. She knew it was a red opal, but this was the first time her mom had told her that it was a gift from a grandma she never knew. Paloma wondered how many more Mexican mysteries would be revealed in the next four weeks. She put the ring on her index finger, but it slipped off easily. She had a lot more growing before it would ever fit.

"I need to write this down." Paloma pulled out a note card and pen. "Ring. Red opal. Mexican grandma. Got it. Continue."

"Someday it will belong to you."

Paloma stopped writing. Her mom's words rang in her ears. She put down the note card and pen. She must have heard the story of how her dad proposed to her mom a hundred times, but she wanted to hear it again.

"Mom?" Paloma said with a yearning her mom knew so well.

"The story again? Don't you ever get sick of it?"

Paloma shook her head.

"All my friends were betting that your dad would propose to me on my graduation day." Paloma's mom started the story they both knew by heart. "We had already been seeing each other for two years. Graduation day came, and there was no ring, no proposal. I was very sad. I thought he had changed his mind about me and—"

"After you had a big dinner with Gramps, Nana, and Dad . . . Get to the good part."

"A good story can't be rushed, young lady."

Paloma groaned.

"Later that night, after a big dinner at my folks' place,

your dad went home, and I was super sad because he hadn't proposed. My mom and I sat up and talked about it. Suddenly, I hear these guitars strumming outside and this wild screeching that sounded like an angry owl mating call. It was past midnight at this point. I go out to the porch, and there are two guys with guitars. Your dad has a bouquet of red roses, and he's singing . . . really badly. All the dogs on the street howled at him. I think someone's car alarm even went off."

Paloma pulled her legs to her chest and laughed. This was her favorite part. Knowing that her dad had a horrible voice just like she did. Once in choir class, her teacher had told her to just pretend to sing with the rest of the group. Isha and Kate never let her live that one down.

"It was horrid singing, but it was the most wonderful night ever because your father got down on one knee, pulled out a box with this beautiful red opal ring, and proposed. The rest is history! The end!"

Paloma clapped. Her mom kissed the top of her head. "You're a nut, you know? Why is it you always want to hear that story?"

Paloma handed the ring back to her mom. "I like knowing that he couldn't sing, either. And I like that the ring is a memory. A memory I can touch that he touched, too."

Her mom turned away like she might cry. Paloma often worried that asking her mom so many questions about her dad was hard on her, but her mom had always said that the day Paloma stopped asking about her father would be worse. At times like these, Paloma had learned to just give her mom a moment.

In the silence between them, Paloma looked out the window. A hummingbird hovered over an orange tree in front of their house. Lulu Pennywhistle had this joke about hummingbirds having to hum because they didn't know the words to any songs. The hummingbird also reminded Paloma of the Frida Kahlo painting where the artist had one dangling from her neck. After a few seconds, her mom started tapping the computer keys again.

"*Valor,*" her mom said. "That's a good word to know in Spanish and English."

"*Valor,*" Paloma repeated, trying to get her mouth to pronounce it right. "*Valor.*" She glanced out the window. Gael and Lizzie were long gone.

Suddenly, Paloma felt ashamed. Her mom had told her that Frida Kahlo was one of her dad's favorite artists. Had she made the right decision not to help Gael and Lizzie find Frida's ring? The peacock ring was special to Frida. It was a memory, too. And if a ring was a memory and it was lost, didn't it mean something about Frida was forgotten?

"Mom, do you know what a churro is?"

Chapter 8

The Fortune-Teller

Paloma and her mom walked the three blocks to Coyoacán's Jardín Centenario to try a churro. The park was full of families taking an afternoon stroll, buying balloons, and eating ice-cream cones. Paloma's head swelled with questions about the peacock ring, Frida Kahlo, and the locked room. Now she just needed to talk to Gael and Lizzie. She hoped they'd forgive her. She wanted to help.

"Look! It's the Fortune-Teller from last night," her mom said. Paloma stopped and watched as the Fortune-Teller called out to tourists in different languages. Some of them stopped to look at her jewelry.

"Let's go see what she's got," her mom said.

"How does a fortune-teller know all those languages?" Paloma pulled out a note card and wrote down the question.

While the Fortune-Teller chatted in a foreign language to a group of tourists, Paloma browsed the beaded necklaces, dangling feathered earrings, and a few silver earrings laid out on the serape. She listened closely, trying to determine the language they spoke. It was full of shushing sounds that Paloma liked.

"Not finding what you're looking for?" asked the Fortune-Teller, startling Paloma.

"Me?" Paloma pointed at herself.

"Yes, you. The girl with the scowl."

Paloma's mom laughed.

"I'm not scowling," Paloma protested. "I'm just thinking." The Fortune-Teller's gray eyes sparkled with specks of green, and she grinned with straight white teeth. "What language were you just speaking to those people?"

"Russian. I speak many languages because I've traveled all over the world, selling rings and telling people's futures. Would you like me to throw the stones for you?"

"Throw stones? No, thanks, but can I see what you have in that box?" Paloma pointed at a wooden box, no bigger than a box of tissues, which was at the Fortune-Teller's side.

"Paloma, don't be so nosy! *Lo siento*," Paloma's mom

said, but the woman waved her apology away and placed the box in front of Paloma.

"These are special rings," she said. "I keep them close because these are only for the serious buyers."

Paloma quickly sat down on the sidewalk across from the Fortune-Teller. "Special rings?" she asked. The Fortune-Teller nodded. "I could be a serious buyer. My grandparents gave me lots of spending money."

A wide smile spread across the Fortune-Teller's face. She opened the box. Inside the box were a dozen shimmering silver rings delicately folded around auburn, turquoise, and emerald gemstones. Paloma reached to grab one from the box but stopped.

"Go ahead, you can touch them, *mi reina.*"

Paloma selected a thick silver ring. It was large and round with intricate designs. She looked closer to see a small face carved into the center of the ring.

"That is the Aztec sun calendar," the Fortune-Teller explained.

"Wow. Let me see it," Paloma's mom said. Paloma handed it to her. A soft smile spread across Paloma's mom's face as she examined the tiny engraved ring. "You know, the first time I met your dad, he wore an Aztec sun calendar medallion. He wore it almost every day, but when you were born, he stopped because whenever he'd hold you, you'd pull it with your tiny hands and try to put it in your mouth . . ."

"I did?" Paloma giggled. It was another detail about her dad she didn't know. She took out a note card and wrote it down.

"He stopped wearing it because he was worried one day you'd pull it off his neck and swallow it," her mom continued. "He always worried so much about those things because you were a very touchy-feely baby . . ." Her mom held the ring between her fingers and trailed off. The Fortune-Teller's eyes moved back and forth between them. Paloma knew they must seem weird. A quiet, dreamy woman stuck in a memory and her note-taking daughter trying desperately to capture the memory with ink.

Even back home, Isha and Kate had told Paloma to cool it with all the note cards. But that's the thing with memories—Paloma never knew when they were going to show up. If she didn't capture them right on the spot, maybe she'd never get the chance again. And she couldn't help but feel she'd already missed too much.

"Well, your rings are beautiful," her mom said, handing the ring back to the Fortune-Teller. "We should move along. We're on a mission to try a churro. Not to buy a ring. Do you know where they sell them?"

"The best ones are made by Camila," the Fortune-Teller answered. "Her stand is in front of the coyote fountain. She has a green umbrella. You can see it from here. Just take this path straight ahead."

As the Fortune-Teller pointed toward the coyote fountain, Paloma tucked her note away and noticed a postcard sticking out beneath the Fortune-Teller's serape. She squinted to get a better look. It was an image of Frida Kahlo and the beginning of a word that started with "FEL." There was no way to mistake Frida's eyes. Professor Breton had said that Coyoacán breathed Frida Kahlo, but was it coincidence that this Fortune-Teller was also a Frida Kahlo fan and sold rings? Lulu didn't believe in coincidences. Moments like these were when Lulu always struck. She used her charm to put people at ease and pressed further for clues. The churros could wait a little longer.

"I totally hope I can buy a ring before we leave, but I'd like a unique ring," Paloma said, handing the box back to the Fortune-Teller.

The Fortune-Teller reached to take the box of rings from her. "What sort of ring? Flower? Leaf? Maybe a silver ring with your birthstone?"

"A peacock ring," Paloma blurted.

"¿*Cómo?* What kind of ring did you say?" the Fortune-Teller asked, almost dropping the box and spilling the rings on her lap. "That—that is a very unusual ring request. Very unusual . . ." she stammered, and steadied the small box. She looked over her rings and closed it. "Have you ever seen one before?"

"We don't have money for fancy rings, Paloma. Let's get

moving, little bird," Paloma's mom jumped in. "A churro is calling our names. That, I can afford."

Paloma frowned. Her mom was ruining her detective work. She stood up reluctantly. "I'll be back," Paloma said as her mom grabbed her by the sleeve. The Fortune-Teller responded with a tight-lipped smile.

As Paloma's mom guided her toward the churros stand, Paloma looked back. The Fortune-Teller was on her cell phone. Who was she talking to? Even the sweet smell of fried dough drifting in the air couldn't get Paloma's mind off the Fortune-Teller's reaction to the mention of a peacock ring. Lulu Pennywhistle was super right when she said that sometimes she had nothing to go by but a "gut feeling." Right now, Paloma's gut told her that there was something suspicious about that Fortune-Teller.

She had to talk to Gael. Fortunately, she spotted him easily. He was sitting on a bench, pencil in hand, his head buried in a sketchbook. Lizzie was nowhere to be seen. Paloma was glad, considering the mood Lizzie had been in when she left the house. Gael looked up and saw Paloma. He closed his sketchbook and tucked it under his arm. She smiled at him, hoping he wasn't upset at how they'd left things.

"Paloma!" Gael stood and rushed over to her. "You came to try a churro?"

Paloma nodded and gazed over the fried golden pastries. "I've never had one, but they smell yummy, like funnel cakes back home." Behind the cart, an older woman handed her mom a small sack filled with churros sprinkled with cinnamon sugar. Paloma snatched a churro from the sack.

"Funnel cakes? I'll have to remember that one," Gael said, handing Paloma a napkin. He leaned closer to her and whispered in her ear, "Does this mean what I think it means?"

"Yes," Paloma whispered back. She gave a side glance to her mom, who was busy talking to the woman selling churros. "I will help you and Lizzie find the peacock ring. And I think we should keep an eye on that Fortune-Teller."

Chapter 9

Portrait of a Father

"Why do you think the Fortune-Teller is involved?" Gael asked as the two walked to Casa Azul. Paloma was shocked by how easy it had been to persuade her mom to let them go to Casa Azul that afternoon while her mom returned home to work. Paloma knew now that whenever she wanted to go somewhere or do something, she'd have Gael ask. Her mom seemed incapable of saying no to cute Gael.

It was Paloma's idea to start the quest for the peacock ring at Casa Azul. Lulu always went to the source of the mystery. Plus, it was the first place Paloma had seen the Fortune-Teller. Paloma wasn't sure, but there could be a connection.

"I can't explain why, except that the Fortune-Teller totally freaked out when I mentioned the peacock ring to her," Paloma explained. "She nearly dropped her box of special rings! And then she was all like, 'What an unusual request.'"

Gael shook his head and chuckled at her exaggerated deep fortune-teller voice.

"Now that I think of it . . ." Gael said. "The Fortune-Teller just showed up in the last few weeks."

Paloma stopped and pulled out a note card and pen. "Tell me more."

"I'm always helping my aunt out with her churro stand . . ." Gael scratched his head. "I hadn't realized it before and it's weird, no? She shows up around the same time Lizzie and I start looking for the ring?"

"The plot thickens!" Paloma clicked her pen and scribbled down Gael's comments. Once she was done, they started walking again.

"Still, you shouldn't have mentioned the ring to her," Gael said finally. "We can't let anyone know we're looking for it. If people find out how valuable it is . . . they may want to search for it, too, and keep it for themselves. Then it will be lost *para siempre*. Forever."

"My bad." Paloma shrugged. "I was in a Lulu Pennywhistle zone."

"*¿Quién?* Who is Lulu?"

"She's this awesome detective in a book series I read. She solves mysteries, and she's totally fearless."

"She is fictional?" Gael asked, and then raised his hands

up to the sky in frustration. "Why are all the bravest people only in stories?"

"The books are fiction, but to me she's like a real person. I've learned a lot from her."

"Good, we will have to be fearless like her."

Paloma nodded. She was glad Gael didn't make fun of her admiration for Lulu Pennywhistle. Kate and Isha had warned her, more than once, that she was starting to sound obsessed when it came to Lulu mysteries.

"Lizzie won't be mad that we're starting the search without her, will she?"

Gael shrugged. "She'll understand."

"She doesn't seem like the understanding type. I mean, she was all huffy-puffy when I said I couldn't help you. And then she stomped off."

"That was *nada*. Nothing. She is a mariachi, you know? Don't ever make a mariachi trumpet player angry." Gael nudged her playfully as they reached the entrance to Casa Azul.

They followed a swarm of tourists through the turnstile and into a large room where several framed portraits hung on the walls. As they entered the room, Paloma noticed a man installing a security camera in the upper corner of the room. Paloma joined Gael in front of a painting titled *Portrait of Don Guillermo Kahlo*.

"This was Frida's father," Gael said. "He had a magnificent mustache."

"Yes, it's a mega mustache," Paloma said about the man's

bushy grayish-brown mustache. The man's thick eyebrows were set over gray eyes that glanced off to the left. Behind him was a large ancient-looking camera. "You know, her name doesn't sound very Mexican."

"That's because her father was from Germany. He came here, worked as a photographer, fell in love with a Mexican woman, and stayed for the rest of his life."

"German father. Mexican mother. Frida is kind of mixed like me."

"What does that mean? 'Kind of mixed'?"

"I'm half-Mexican and half-German, too. My dad was from Mexico. My mom's family was originally from Germany. She always says she comes from 'good Kansas German stock.'"

"This is the first time you've mentioned your dad," Gael said. "Why wasn't he at the reception last night? Are your parents divorced?"

Paloma took a deep breath and folded her arms across her chest. "My father died when I was three years old."

Gael stepped back and placed his hand over his heart. "*Lo siento*, Paloma!" He covered his face with his hands and rattled off a dramatic Spanish apology. None of which Paloma understood, but she got the gist. "*¡Qué pena! Perdóname*, Paloma. I'm a dork! *¡Perdón!*"

"It's okay, Gael. You didn't know."

"I am *idiota*. I don't know how to say that in English."

"It's almost the same in English, but you're not an idiot," Paloma said, and sighed.

"I think you deserve a hug now—is that okay?"

"Okay." Paloma shrugged. Gael took her in a warm, tight hug. He smelled like cinnamon-sweet churros.

"So sorry that you don't have your dad," he whispered before letting her go. Gael removed one of the leather cords from around his neck. He held it out to her. "I want you to have this. It will protect you."

"From what?" Paloma dipped her head down to let Gael loop it around her neck. She held the tiny silver medallion in her hands and examined it.

"It's an Aztec eagle warrior," Gael explained. "They were soldiers who defended their people from enemies."

Paloma thought about the Aztec calendar medallion that her father wore. Her mom had told her that he wore it all the time. Now Paloma wondered if it had been a gift from a friend, too. Paloma pressed the medallion between her fingers. She hoped to draw out a memory of being a child pulling on her dad's medallion. She stood there for a second with her eyes closed, but no memory came.

"Thank you," she finally said to Gael, who watched her with kind brown eyes.

She was desperate to change the topic. She didn't want pity. Paloma pointed back to the painting. Along the bottom part of the portrait were Spanish words written in reddish cursive. "What does it say here?"

"Frida writes: 'I painted my father, Wilhelm Kahlo, of Hungarian-German origin, artist-photographer, in a way that shows his character as intelligent, generous, and valiant because he suffered from an illness called *epilepsia*'—I'm not sure how to say that in English, but it's an illness that—"

Paloma looked closer at the words. "I think it means 'epilepsy.' He had epilepsy."

Gael nodded. "Yes, that's it. Anyway, it says that he also fought against Hitler. She signs it, 'with adoration,'" Gael continued. "She loved him very much. You can tell by how she painted him that she truly loved him."

Paloma's gaze moved away from the painting of Frida's father to a blank spot on the wall. In that empty white space, she imagined a canvas. And on the canvas, she'd paint her own father. First, she'd sketch him. He would be sitting upright, very formally like Frida's father. But Paloma's father would be smiling, showing off his perfect white teeth. Then she'd fill in his face with paint the hue of caramel candy. She'd use the darkest black color she could find for his short hair. In the portrait, she'd paint him in a blue button-down shirt with the silver Aztec calendar necklace around his neck. Her mom had said he'd worn it every day. This was important to him, so it should be in the portrait, too, Paloma thought. In the background, she'd paint the sun pyramid from the photograph her mom framed.

If she painted this portrait, would people know that she also loved him? Would they know, by just looking at it, how much she missed him?

"Paloma?" Gael put his hand on her shoulder. "Are you okay?"

Paloma let the portrait fade away. She tucked a loose strand of hair behind her ear. "I'm fine. I was just thinking about how we're going to find this ring. Where do we even start?"

Gael narrowed his eyes at her, unconvinced. "I can give you another hug. I think I've upset you about your father."

"No more time for hugs. We have a mystery to solve," she said, ignoring his rejected look. "Show me where the locked room was found. Lulu always starts with the obvious."

"It's upstairs, near Frida's studio," Gael answered.

Paloma took one more look around the gallery. It was just four white walls, but long ago it had been Frida's living room. She lived here with her sisters and parents, and later with her husband. Now the walls were covered with family portraits. In those paintings, Paloma could see the love Frida had for her family and the family tree that connected her to Europe and Mexico forever. Paloma only had her mom and her mom's family in Kansas. And although she knew that she was loved, Paloma couldn't help but believe there was a whole other side of her family tree that she didn't know anything about. If her dad had lived, would she have cousins, uncles, and aunts in Mexico? Would she feel connected to the spirit of this place the way Frida did?

"Ready to find some clues, Paloma?" Gael asked.

Paloma nodded. "Finding clues is my specialty!"

Chapter 10

The Secret Room

"It's. A. Bathroom," Paloma said, shaking her head in disbelief. She and Gael stared into the small tiled bathroom, guarded only by a knee-high wire strung along the doorway to keep visitors from entering.

"It's a secret room," Gael said. "This is where Diego hid many of her things."

"It's. A. Bathroom."

"Stop saying that," Gael whispered. "This room is important. Everything was found here." A few tourists passed by, barely giving the small bathroom a glance.

"No one even cares that it's here," Paloma said.

"*Exacto*," Gael said with sudden urgency. "They have no clue what this room contained, but we do."

Paloma's eyes strayed to a framed sign posted next to the bathroom. "What does that say?"

Gael leaned in. "It says that over three hundred pieces of Frida's personal items were discovered here. It also says that many of the items are on display in the exhibition space."

"Exhibition space?" Paloma said. "That sounds promising."

"It was open last night," Gael scoffed. "You probably didn't see it because you were too busy making googly eyes at Tavo Farill."

Paloma's mouth dropped open. Gael laughed.

"Googly eyes? Who taught you that?" Paloma asked. Suddenly, a loud swarm of tourists rushed past Paloma and Gael down the narrow hallway, knocking Paloma into the wire. Gael grabbed her arm, helping her to get her balance. "Sheesh!" Paloma said. "Share the road, people."

"It's a tour group," Gael said. "French, I bet. They love Frida."

"Let's follow them. Maybe they're going to the exhibit space, too."

Paloma and Gael quickly joined the French-speaking tour group. The group moved through Frida's dayroom, where skeleton marionettes dangled from Frida's small bed, and small porcelain dolls sat on a shelf. The tour continued into another small room at the farthest end of Frida's home. Paloma glanced inside. Another twin-size bed, covered with a lacy white blanket and pillow, was positioned to the side of the room. She tugged at Gael's sleeve.

"Why did Frida have two bedrooms?" she asked, stepping through the doorway. Gael followed her. The room had no windows. It was dark but was illuminated by a few lamps. "I want two bedrooms."

"Careful what you ask for, Paloma," Gael whispered. "Frida needed two bedrooms. I thought I heard Tavo tell you last night about the bus accident she was in, no?"

Paloma nodded, resisting the urge to call him an eavesdropper.

"After the accident, she had many surgeries. She couldn't leave her bed, so that was when she began to paint. She had one room where she could lie down and paint. The other room was for sleeping. In the end, she died in her sleep," Gael said.

"She died here?" Paloma asked. Gael nodded and gestured to a headless frog-shaped sculpture atop a wood dresser.

"Her ashes are inside that urn," Gael said.

Paloma gave Gael a look of disbelief and pointed at the urn. "Are you telling me that Frida's ashes are inside that ugly frog thingy?"

Gael nodded.

The frog urn was the color of red clay and was no larger than the vase Paloma's mom had just used for calla lilies back at home. Paloma stepped aside and let a few tourists slip past her to take a photo of the urn. Their cameras clicked and flashed a dozen times. She gazed around the room, and waited for the tourists to leave. Once they had the room to themselves, Paloma rummaged through her bag for note cards and a pen.

"That. Is. A. Major. Detail. Why didn't you tell me about her urn before?"

"Sorry, Miss Lupe Purplewhistle," Gael joked. "I didn't realize it was a major detail."

Paloma growled. "It's Lulu Pennywhistle," she corrected him. She leaned against another wire barrier to get as close to the urn as she could, and raised her phone to take a couple of pictures. But then she stopped. Through the phone screen, she saw the red clay sculpture with its little frog hands and skinny frog legs and felt strangely ashamed. She lowered her phone.

"What's wrong, Paloma? *¿Qué pasa?* You look sad." Gael took her hand.

"This is Frida's final resting place," Paloma said softly. "She's inside that ugly sculpture. I just feel like . . . it's dumb, I guess, but I feel like I should say a little prayer or something."

Gael nodded. "What do you do when you visit your dad's grave?"

Paloma was stunned by the question, but realized Gael had a point. This urn was like Frida's gravestone. "I—I," she stammered. She and her mom visited her dad's gravestone three times a year: on his birthday, the anniversary of his death, and on Father's Day. She suspected her mom went more often, though. Sometimes her mom would leave Paloma with friends or family and return in a quiet mood with a special treat, as if she felt guilty for something. "I say a prayer, and then I just talk to him about things."

"*¿Cómo?* Like what?"

"School, my friends, and stuff like that." Paloma shrugged. "Sometimes, I even tell him about the latest Lulu Pennywhistle book I'm reading."

"You should do that," Gael said. "Talk to her."

Paloma looked around the room one more time to make sure they were still alone.

"*Hola*, Frida . . ." Paloma started. "I really like your home. It—" She stopped, looked over at Gael. She was unsure of what else to say.

Gael gave Paloma an encouraging nod. "You're doing awesome."

Paloma faced the urn again.

"It means a lot to be here because you were one of my dad's favorite artists. I don't know if he ever visited Coyoacán, but I think he would have liked it. I like it. Anyway, I hope you know that you're very popular. People even take pictures of your urn. It's a big hit. Congrats on that," Paloma said. "I want you to also know that I'm sorry that your peacock ring is missing. Don't worry, we're going to find it for you."

Paloma stepped back from the urn. "Rest in peace, Frida."

"*Muy padre*, Paloma," Gael said with a wide, satisfied smile. "Very cool."

"Thanks," Paloma said. "No time to waste. Show me the gallery."

The art gallery was dark. The only lighting in the room came from inside large glass displays filled with faceless mannequins dressed in colorful skirts, silk headpieces, and ruffled blouses. Gael motioned for Paloma to follow him into the next room, where they passed Frida's crutches, leather back brace, and prosthetic leg all on display. Paloma gasped at the strappy leather back brace with large metal buckles. Then Gael led her into the last room in the gallery, where Frida's jewelry glimmered from display cases.

"This is where her peacock ring should be," Gael said. Paloma's brown eyes skimmed over the display cases full of silver and gold rings and necklaces with turquoise and other exotic stones.

"Maybe Diego hid her things away because back then they didn't have good security in place to protect from robbery? I mean, now they have cameras." She pointed up toward the ceiling where a small lens watched them. "I also saw a man installing one inside the museum. But before now, what sort of security did they have?"

"Frida use to have a pet monkey and a couple of hairless dogs," Gael answered. "That's about it."

"Be serious," Paloma said, rolling her eyes. She paced the

room and ran through everything she knew so far. "We know Diego hid these things in the bathroom . . ." she started. "But what if there was another locked room somewhere? Another secret room where he hid other items that were more personal and worth more . . . like the peacock ring? Maybe he died before he had the chance to tell anyone about it. Or maybe he never wanted anyone to know."

"If there was another locked room, don't you think someone would have found it by now?"

Paloma shrugged. "Maybe not. It took them fifty years to discover one secret room. We can't afford to let the adults take another fifty years to open another—"

"If there is another," Gael added, rubbing his medallion between his fingers.

"That's right," Paloma admitted. "It's just a theory right now, but we only have a couple of weeks to solve this mystery before Frida's birthday."

"Where do we start?"

"In cases like this, Lulu Pennywhistle always applies the POE."

"POE?"

"Process of elimination," Paloma said, punching the air above her with her pen. "We must search Casa Azul for another secret room left behind by Diego. If we don't find it, we can disprove that theory and move on to the Fortune-Teller. No time to waste."

Paloma marched out of the dark gallery into the sunlight

beaming into Frida's patio and garden. In the daylight, the courtyard hummed with activity. Some tourists lined up for refreshments at an outdoor café, while others popped in and out of a gift shop. A few people took turns snapping selfies in front of a yellow-and-red pyramid structure. A man dressed in a police uniform strolled the garden, singing to himself.

"Time for a *limonada*," Gael said, marching past Paloma and toward the line of people at the café.

"*¿Limonada?*" Paloma exclaimed, throwing her hands up in frustration. "Lulu doesn't stop for *limonada*!" Gael found a place in line. He smirked at her from across the patio.

Paloma joined him, but she wasn't happy about it. They had just ordered two lemonades, when Gael nudged her hard. Paloma glared at him and nudged him back.

"Is that who I think it is?" Gael asked in a serious tone. Paloma followed his gaze to the right of the café. Through a transparent tarp that enclosed the café on one side, a slender man in a suit strolled between the tarp and the courtyard's cement wall.

"Mr. Farill?" Paloma said. "I wonder if Tavo is with him . . ." She trailed off as the woman behind the counter presented two lemonades. Gael was suddenly no longer at her side. She spun around and saw him adjusting his knit cap over his ears and darting away from her. "Gael? What about the *limonada*?"

He motioned toward the museum. "*Baño*. Bathroom," he said, scurrying across the patio.

"Okay, I guess I'll pay," Paloma muttered. She dug through her pockets for a few Mexican pesos. "Go ahead, let the Kansas girl pay for the *limonada* that *you* wanted," Paloma continued, ignoring the confused look of the woman behind the counter.

"Allow me to get those for you, Paloma," Mr. Farill said, suddenly appearing next to her. He handed a couple of bills to the woman.

"Thanks." Paloma smiled and stepped out of the line, holding the two lemonades.

"Is your mom with you?" he asked.

"No, she's at home working. I came here with a friend, but he . . ." She looked back toward the museum. "He went to take care of something."

"He?" Mr. Farill said. "It's not my son is it? Tavo is supposed to be helping his mom, but maybe he came here instead?" He raised his eyebrows a few times, and it made Paloma blush.

"No, it's just my Spanish tutor."

"A Spanish tutor! That's great, Paloma." Mr. Farill grinned. "You're taking advantage of everything Coyoacán has to offer. That is superb."

"Thanks." She nodded. "It was my mom's idea. Are you here to see Frida's artwork? Is there another exhibit behind the cafeteria?" Paloma asked.

"Over there? No. There's nothing there. I got lost looking for the gift shop," Mr. Farill said. "I'm only here on orders from my wife. She's helping with plans for Frida's birthday party. She needed me to pick something up. I'll make sure to give your mom an invitation for the party when you come over tomorrow night."

"Muchas gracias," Paloma chirped.

Mr. Farill answered with an impressed smile. "Your accent is excellent! Please tell your mom hello for me," he said, giving Paloma a quick nod. As he sauntered across the patio and out the museum exit, a whiff of his peppery cologne remained. Paloma couldn't help but think how cool it would be to have a dad who wore fancy gray suits, nice-smelling cologne, and showed up out of nowhere to pay for lemonade.

When Gael reappeared, she shoved a plastic cup of lemonade at him.

"What was that, Gael?"

"Sorry." He winced. He took a sip of lemonade. "What did Farill say to you? Why was he here?"

"He's helping out with Frida's birthday party."

"Behind the cafeteria?" Gael asked, walking toward the tarp where they first saw Mr. Farill. "Are there more offices back here? Bathrooms?" Gael mumbled something in Spanish as he found an opening in the tarp and walked through it. Paloma stepped through it as well, expecting someone to stop her, but no one did. They continued down a long, narrow passageway between the cafeteria and the outer wall of Frida's courtyard. The two of them walked until the path stopped at a large old tree with low, thick branches. On the ground were a couple of fresh cigarette butts. Gael frowned and squashed the cigarette butts with his shoes. Paloma eyed the large tree and its dense branches. A wind swept through, and the branches swayed just enough for Paloma to catch a glimpse of a wooden door.

"There's something behind here," Paloma said. She placed her lemonade on the ground and pulled back a few branches. She squeezed between the tree's branches and the outer courtyard wall and stumbled. As she got back up, she faced the old wooden door, locked with a rusty metal padlock.

"Gael, I may have found something!" Paloma yelled.

"Estoy aquí," he answered, ducking under a tree branch to join her. "I'm here. I see it."

They stared at the door in complete silence. Paloma couldn't help but feel like she was looking at a second secret room, locked by Frida's husband, Diego Rivera. She clutched Gael's arm.

"This could be it," she whispered.

"Or it could be an old mop room," Gael said, grabbing the lock to inspect it. "It's ancient." He jiggled the doorknob to see if it would open. It didn't. "Do you think Mr. Farill saw it?"

Paloma shrugged. "I don't think so. He said he was looking for the gift shop."

Gael scanned the ground and grabbed a rock. He struck the lock with it. The lock didn't budge.

"What are you doing?" Paloma exclaimed. "Are you trying to get security called on us?"

Gael tossed the rock down. "You're right. We're going to have to come back when the museum is closed. At midnight."

"No way, José! My mom would never be down with that," Paloma said. "Your cute dimples aren't going to convince her to let me out at midnight."

"You're going to have to sneak out— Wait a minute! Did you say my dimples are cute?"

Paloma rolled her eyes. "Midnight is a no-go."

"Look around you, Paloma. This place is full of tourists. It's the only way to find out what's in that room," Gael said. "Lulu Pennywhistle would do it."

Paloma felt as though she'd just been squashed like those cigarette butts on the ground. How dare he use Lulu against her. Yet, she knew he was right. The entire museum and courtyard buzzed with visitors, and there was a police officer walking around. It would be easier to search the locked room when the museum was empty. But at midnight? She hated the idea of sneaking out. What if they were caught and thrown into jail? Did they throw kids in jail in Mexico? Most of all, she hated going behind her mom's back.

Still, Paloma's mind raced with possibilities. What if the

door revealed a secret room full of Mexican treasures? What if the peacock ring was inside? Mystery solved! Game over! Done! Her mom told her to embrace new opportunities in Mexico, right?

Paloma nodded. "Okay, let's do it."

Chapter 11

Too Early for Trumpets

The next morning, a trumpet blared outside Paloma's bedroom window. Her mom burst through the door, startling Paloma awake.

"It's a *serenata*!" her mom squealed, clapping her hands as she pushed aside the curtains and opened the window. An upbeat guitar rhythm and trumpet melody filled the room.

"What's all that racket? It's too early for trumpets." Paloma pulled the bed comforter over her head. "Turn down the volume," she barked.

"Your friends are serenading you, Paloma. Get up and see."

Paloma rubbed her eyes open. "*¡No me gusta!*" She sat up and scowled at the window. Being grumpy in the morning was sort of her thing, but this morning deserved an extra dose of grouch. All night, Paloma tossed and turned in bed, unsure of how she'd climb out her bedroom window and sneak out the front gate that night. What had she gotten herself into?

"Get over here, grouchy bird. Come wave to them," Paloma's mom called to her from the windowsill. Paloma was not ready to leave her bed, but watching her mom bounce her head with the music softened her mood until she felt like the cottony blankets she wanted to hide under all morning. She slowly rose up out of bed and walked over to the window. Her mom wrapped an arm around Paloma's waist.

Paloma gazed at the tree branches she'd have to climb down tonight. It suddenly looked very far from the ground. A lump formed in her throat.

"Isn't this cool?" her mom asked, never taking her eyes off Gael and Lizzie outside the front gate below. Gael sang and strummed away on a blue guitar. Lizzie joined in with her silver trumpet. A man who was sweeping the street stopped and sang along. Her mom laughed, and Paloma couldn't help but giggle, too. In return, Gael sent up the sweetest dimpled smile. Once the song was over, Paloma's mom hurried down the stairs to open the gate for them. "I love Mexico! This is so amazing!"

Paloma splashed water on her face and brushed her hair. What did this serenade mean? The only other time she had heard about a serenade was when her father proposed to her mother. Was Gael proposing? She was only twelve—way too young to get married!

She pulled on a T-shirt, yoga pants, and the Aztec eagle warrior medallion. Once she got downstairs to the living room, Gael and Lizzie were already inside. Her mom rambled on about how much she adored that song and what a nice surprise it had been to wake up to music. While her mom raved, Gael stole a look at Paloma. No doubt, she liked Gael. She thought he was sweet, like the sort of boy who would decorate her locker on her birthday. Still, she wasn't ready for a marriage proposal. She had things to accomplish.

Lizzie cleared her throat, and her eyes met Paloma's.

"*Hola*, Kansas," Lizzie said, stepping toward her. Paloma braced herself for a slug in the arm or something. Lizzie hadn't been exactly happy with her the last time they'd talked. Instead, Lizzie gave her a quick kiss on the cheek. "It was Gael's idea. Hope you liked it."

"What's not to like about a trumpet blowing through your window at eight in the morning?"

Paloma's mom gave her a don't-be-little-miss-grouch look. Gael stepped closer and planted a kiss on her cheek, too. "*Buenos días*, Paloma. You look very awake."

"Blame the trumpet." Paloma shrugged, not feeling alert at all.

"Ignore her. Come to the table, and I'll get you some juice," Paloma's mom said, pulling out a chair from the dining room table for Lizzie. "I have croissants and papaya." Paloma's mom rushed off to the kitchen but not before slipping Paloma a glare that told her to be nice. The three kids took a seat at the table.

"So are you going to propose to me or what, Gael?" Paloma said, causing Gael to turn red. Lizzie laughed and clapped her hands. "That's what a serenade means, right?"

"Sometimes," Lizzie said, and playfully ruffled Gael's knit hat. Gael winced at her and readjusted it. "We also serenade people on birthdays or if we're thankful for something," Lizzie explained. "It was Gael's idea to serenade you. I went along with it because he told me that you found a secret room at Casa Azul and you're going with us to check it out tonight. *Gracias*, Kansas."

"De nada," Paloma said. She wiped her forehead in an exaggerated gesture of relief. "I'm just glad Gael isn't proposing to me. I'm too young," she teased. "I still have to go to high school and college."

Gael slunk down lower into his chair and shook his head. "No, it's just to thank you for helping us," he said in a whisper so that Paloma's mom wouldn't hear from the kitchen. "I'm too young for marriage, too. I have to become a famous artist."

Lizzie leaned closer to Paloma. "Sneaking out tonight shows a lot of *valor*."

"Thanks." Paloma smiled. No one had ever called her brave before. Her friends back home in Kansas mostly called her grumpy face, worrywart, smarty-pants, and nosy butt, but never courageous. Still, Paloma was nervous about sneaking out of the house tonight. She couldn't back out now. Not after Lizzie had just said she had courage.

"I don't understand how we're going to get into Casa Azul, though," Paloma said. "I'm not cool with breaking in."

"We won't be breaking in exactly . . ." Lizzie said. "My mariachi band is practicing there tonight for Frida's birthday celebration. When everyone leaves, I'm going to unlock the back door."

"What about the security cameras? I saw they had some inside the exhibit space and museum. There's no way I can get caught. My mom will freak out."

Lizzie gave a slight shrug. "Those cameras are new and mostly just inside the museum right now. And the ones outside in the courtyard won't get a good look at our faces if we wear a mask or hat."

Paloma liked how confident Lizzie sounded. "I don't really keep masks around, so I guess I can wear a baseball cap."

"That will work." Lizzie nodded. "Look, you just focus on climbing down the tree and getting to the front gate. We'll worry about the rest."

Paloma tugged on the medallion around her neck and looked back toward the kitchen, where her mom hummed the song that Gael and Lizzie had just performed. She had to admit, Lizzie's reassurance calmed her.

"You know, since I'll be at Tavo's house tonight for dinner, I was thinking I could talk to him about the peacock ring. He knows some serious stuff about Frida. He might be able to help us. I can ask him."

Gael and Lizzie both winced.

"It's not a good idea to include Tavo," Lizzie said. "If he tells his father about what we're doing, his parents will take it over."

"It's true," Gael added. "His parents are very involved with the museum. We have to keep this between us. You understand, right?"

Paloma knew they were right. They couldn't afford to let the parents or any adult get involved. How many times had Lulu Pennywhistle had her cases sabotaged by some know-it-all adult brandishing a fancy "detective" badge? Or a police investigator who thought he was smarter just because he was older than Lulu and had fancy credentials framed on his wall?

"Don't worry. I know how to keep a secret," Paloma answered, and pretended to zip her lips. Gael and Lizzie seemed satisfied with that.

"I hear Tavo has a big house with a pool and lots of fancy art on the walls. It's like a museum! You should definitely plan to take lots of pictures," Lizzie said just as Paloma's mom showed up at the table with a tray of warm croissants and chopped papaya. "What time is your dinner tonight?"

"Mr. Farill has arranged for a driver to pick us up here at the house at six," Paloma's mom said, scooping a spoonful of papaya onto Lizzie's plate. "So we can't be late, Paloma."

"You say that like I'm always late." Paloma scowled.

"You are. There's always a flower to pin in your hair at the last minute or a change of shoes or the wrong scarf holding you up," her mom said while Gael and Lizzie chuckled.

"*Sí*, Paloma. You can't be late tonight," Gael said with an amused grin. "It's an important night."

Paloma knew he wasn't talking about the dinner.

Chapter 12

Mystery for Dinner

The gray BMW arrived outside their home at six. Paloma
wore a denim shirt with white pants, and a pair of sandals.
She pinned a yellow flower in her hair. As they drove to the
Farills' house, they passed a hundred small homes until bigger homes surrounded with high iron gates appeared.

When they finally reached Tavo's neighborhood, they
stopped at a security checkpoint, where one officer collected
the driver's ID and another scanned under the car and
inside the trunk with a long wand. Paloma had never been to
a neighborhood where visitors had to pass through a checkpoint. Airport security was easier to get through! Paloma
was ready to hand over her purse and shoes for inspection,
when the guards waved them through another set of gates.

As the entrance opened ahead, Paloma noticed a taxi pulling up behind them. The taxi stopped, and the security guards hovered around it. In the brief moment between Paloma's driver moving forward and the gate closing behind them, she thought she saw a kid with a black knit hat pop his head out of the back window to speak to the security guard. Paloma could swear it was Gael, but when the car drove forward, she lost sight of the boy in the taxi. What would Gael be doing here? Did he also live in the neighborhood? And if so, Tavo must know him. As the car drove up the tree-lined driveway to the mansion, Paloma decided she would definitely ask Tavo tonight.

And it was Tavo himself who opened the car door for Paloma and her mom when the car rolled to a stop. It had only been two days since Paloma last saw him, but somehow with all the excitement of a mystery and Gael, she'd forgotten how super dreamy he was. Paloma wanted to be sure to get a selfie with him so she could make her friends in Kansas swoon with jealousy.

"*Bienvenidos* to our humble home!" He grinned, and Paloma laughed. There was nothing humble about his place. It was a three-story white stone mansion with at least a dozen stairs leading up to the dark wood front doors. The yard was decorated with an elaborate fountain and dotted with manicured trees and rosebushes.

When they entered the house, Paloma's mom almost slipped on the gray marbled floors. Tavo caught her by the arm and winced.

"I forgot to warn you about the floors," he said. "I slip all the time because I like to run around in socks, but I have to stop doing that because my mom says one of these days I'm going to crack my head open."

"Gross!" Paloma said, shaking her head.

Tavo chuckled. "My bad. No cracking-head jokes before dinner. Got it." He led them into the main living room, where Tavo's parents sauntered down a beautiful long staircase to greet them. To Paloma, they looked like models straight out of an advertisement for a luxury yacht or something else she was sure she couldn't afford.

"*¡Bienvenidos!* Welcome!" Mrs. Farill exclaimed.

"Dinner is almost ready," Mr. Farill said after their greetings of kisses. "While we wait for the finishing touches, why don't we give you a tour of the house? Let's start with the patio. You can say hello to Ninja and Matador, our purebred German shepherds. True beauties but worthless guard dogs."

Mrs. Farill quickly locked arms with Paloma's mom and followed Mr. Farill out of the living room and onto the patio. As the parents walked ahead, Tavo offered his arm and Paloma took it.

"You look really pretty today," he said. Paloma felt her whole face flush. "After dinner, I want to show you something downstairs, okay?"

After a tour of the house that included a den decorated with several paintings, a home theater, and a gym that overlooked the lap pool and patio, they enjoyed a feast of chicken mole, a traditional Mexican dish of spicy chili and chocolate sauce drizzled over chicken. Paloma took several pictures throughout the evening, including a few photos of the mole. During dinner, Paloma's mom and the Farills discussed her fellowship project in Coyoacán, but spent the majority of the evening talking about the upcoming party at Casa Azul for Frida Kahlo's birthday. Mrs. Farill boasted that many of Mexico's most famous artists and most prominent families would be there. The dress code for the party was formal, and everyone was encouraged to wear fancy masks.

"Whose idea was it to make it a masquerade?" Paloma's mom asked. "That sounds like so much fun." Mrs. Farill and Tavo both pointed at Mr. Farill and then laughed that they'd done it at the same time.

Mr. Farill shrugged. "Guilty as charged," he said with a playful grin. "I thought it would be a unique way to celebrate Frida. Everyone shows up in a mask, and you're not really sure who is who."

"Yes, but it was a very last-minute idea . . ." Mrs. Farill said. She shook a finger at her husband. "Two weeks ago, the invitations were ready to go to the printer. Suddenly, he comes up with this idea. I loved it, but I wish he'd come up with it earlier. Anyway, I had to change the invitations to add *baile de máscaras.*"

"The invitations turned out fine," he said. "You did an amazing job."

"I heard there will be mariachis like at the reception the other night?" Paloma asked, thinking about Lizzie's group practicing tonight at Casa Azul.

"Absolutely! There will be several mariachi groups playing throughout the evening. We will also have folkloric dancers." Mrs. Farill beamed. "Only the best for Frida!"

Once the last bites of chicken mole were taken and coffee had been served, Mr. Farill apologized and returned to his office to work. Paloma's mom and Mrs. Farill went out to the patio with their coffees to chat more about the upcoming party. Tavo and Paloma stayed with them for a few minutes before he invited Paloma downstairs to play a game of billiards.

Paloma followed him down a spiraling staircase to a large room lined with built-in bookshelves. Off to the side was the billiards table. And to the right was a glass door that led to a room with wall-to-wall wine bottles. Inside the wine cellar, Paloma could see a small painting hanging above a silver high-top table with three silver stools around it. Tavo jiggled the doorknob.

"This room is off-limits," he said. "It's always locked, but I know where the key is . . ." He shot Paloma a devilish grin. "Do you dare me?"

"Double-dare," Paloma said, to play along.

Tavo walked to a bookshelf and pulled out a book. He opened the book and removed a key. He flashed it in front of

Paloma with a satisfied smile. "Ta-da!" he exclaimed, and unlocked the cellar. "Open sesame!"

Paloma followed Tavo into the cellar. He disappeared behind a shelf and came back out with a dark bottle in his hand.

"This bottle is worth five thousand dollars." Tavo juggled it around.

Paloma shuddered. "Whatever you do, don't drop it. That's like our apartment's rent for four months."

Tavo threw it up in the air and caught it. Paloma rolled her eyes. Why did boys have to be so obnoxious sometimes? Tavo laughed and returned the bottle to its shelf.

"And how much is that creepy painting worth?" Paloma asked. The painting on the wall was of an old wrinkled man wearing a slouchy yellow hat. Around his neck he wore a white furry collar, but what spooked Paloma most was the uneven eyes.

"Ick." Paloma shuddered. "It's one of those harlequin clowns, right? Gives me the creeps."

"Not a Picasso fan?"

"It's a Picasso?" Paloma spotted the signature along the bottom right of the painting. "A real one? People pay millions for Picassos, right?"

"Sure, but did you know that one of Frida Kahlo's paintings was sold for nearly eight million dollars in New York City a few years ago?"

"Whoa, way to go, Frida," Paloma said, punching her hand in the air. "Too bad she's not alive to enjoy it. If she were, she'd probably buy more hummingbird necklaces. You can *never* have enough of those."

Tavo chuckled. "I'm impressed," he said. "You were really paying attention the night of the reception."

"I went back to Casa Azul yesterday, too," Paloma said.

"My dad said he saw you there. You were with your Spanish tutor. How's that going? You know, I could have helped you with Spanish if you wanted. You wouldn't have to pay me or anything."

"It was my mom's idea. She signed me up with a tutoring program, and I start Introduction to Mexican Art and Culture and my Spanish class later this week," Paloma said, adding a gagging gesture.

"Can you get out of it?"

"I wish!" Paloma said. "Honestly, I don't mind the tutoring, but summer school is boring. It's worse than watching people floss."

Tavo laughed.

"My tutor isn't bad, though. He's nice. Maybe you know him . . . His name is Gael Castillo. He's our age, and I think he might live around here. I thought I saw him in a taxi behind us as we pulled up to security."

Tavo shook his head slowly. "Doesn't sound familiar, but I'm only here during the summers." Tavo shrugged.

Paloma bit down on her lip. Maybe the kid she saw in the taxi wasn't Gael. It's not like he was the only boy who wore a black knit hat. Paloma shook her head at her wild imagination.

"Do you think it'd be all right to take a picture of the creepy Picasso?"

Tavo clapped like it was the best idea he'd heard all year. "A selfie in my dad's 'off-limits' cellar. That'll show him, right?" He excitedly pulled his cell phone from his back pocket.

Paloma smiled but suddenly felt sorry for Tavo. The first night they met, after Lizzie played that sad melody on the trumpet, Tavo had called himself a lonely boy. Now she could see why. Tavo was being dragged from Spain to Arizona and back to Mexico at his parents' whim. He probably barely had time to make any true friends.

Tavo nudged her. "Ready?" He snapped a few selfies of them standing at the tall table with the Picasso painting directly behind them.

"Send it to me," Paloma said. She recited her number.

"Sending it now," he said as he tapped his phone.

Paloma glanced at the photo as it appeared. A small gold coin sat on the cocktail table in front of them. She hadn't even noticed it before. She looked closer at the picture and also spotted a little green light coming from the ceiling above the painting. It was a security camera.

"Tavo!" She pointed up at the green light. "Your dad is probably watching us right now."

Tavo winked at her. "The cameras are filming, but he's not watching. He hasn't figured out how to do that on the computer yet. I know because I set it up for him. He has no clue how it works."

Paloma was amazed that she only noticed the gold coin and the camera in the picture when the whole time they were in front of her face. How many times did her mom lecture her about too much time spent behind the phone and not enough paying attention to what was actually around her? She hated to admit it, but her mom was right.

On the ride home, Paloma watched her mom doze in the backseat. She murmured strange things like "I have to finish my paper," when raindrops started to pound against the car windows.

"Of course, it has to rain," Paloma said out loud, and shook her head. As if sneaking out of the house by climbing down a tree wasn't tough enough. Just then, her phone vibrated. It was a text from Gael.

How was dinner?

Paloma sent a thumbs-up emoji. She followed it with a bunch of photos she'd taken of her plate of chicken mole, the home theater, the pool, the selfie with Tavo, and the two adorable German shepherds.

Her phone vibrated again.

Do not chicken out tonight. Rain or shine.

She wasn't going to chicken out. They needed to see this secret room. Paloma's mom was so tired, she'd sleep through anything. Paloma wasn't sure if she'd ever get a better chance to sneak away. No, the mission had to happen tonight.

Chapter 13

Midnight at Casa Azul

Ten minutes before midnight, the rain stopped and the only sound Paloma could hear was her mom's snoring vibrating through the house. It was a high-pitched wheeze that sounded like the vacuum cleaner trying to suck up a stray scarf or sock that Paloma left on the floor. Once her mom started snoring like that, nothing woke her.

Dressed in black jeans, sneakers, a long-sleeved shirt, a rain jacket, and a baseball cap, Paloma crept quietly out her open bedroom window. As she latched on to a wet tree branch and found her footing on another, she could already see Gael and Lizzie waiting for her beyond the front gate. Gael waved, and for a second, Paloma almost waved back but then remembered she was nearly twenty feet off the ground. Polite greetings would have to wait. Within a few minutes, Paloma was on the ground and out the gate. She closed it slowly behind her and locked it with her key.

Paloma grinned at Gael and Lizzie, who were dressed head to toe in black. Lizzie had her hair in two tight braids and held her black trumpet case strapped over her shoulder like it was a bow and arrow.

"Everything is set," Gael whispered. "Lizzie left the door unlocked after mariachi practice."

"*Vamos.* Let's go," Lizzie said in a soft but urgent voice. Gael and Paloma followed after her. They walked through the dark uneven streets, lit only by a few streetlamps. Paloma took a good look around. Coyoacán was beautiful at midnight. The golden glow from the streetlamps made the cobbled streets look like they were paved with magic shiny stones. She felt very much like Lulu Pennywhistle out on an adventure. Her heart pounded fast.

"The dinner with Tavo looked awesome," Gael whispered. "I especially liked the photo of the chicken mole."

"I knew you'd like that one," Paloma said. "Did you see the Picasso painting? I sent you a picture from their wine cellar—"

"A real Picasso?" Lizzie asked over her shoulder, never missing a step forward toward Casa Azul.

"I think so," Paloma said. "It was signed."

"Cool," Gael said.

"And before we left, Mrs. Farill invited my mom and me to go with them to Mexico City on Sunday to see more art by Frida and Diego."

"You're going to see Tavo again?" Gael asked, keeping a quick pace beside her.

"I guess so. I can learn more about Frida, you know. Gather more clues," Paloma said, worried if Gael was a little bit jealous. Gael shrugged and stayed quiet until they arrived on Londres Street.

Lizzie steered them past Casa Azul's front entrance on Londres. She stopped in front of a side door on Allende. From the golden glow of a streetlamp, Paloma could make out the Mexican flag and another flag with blue stripes and a yellow circle painted on the door.

"Let's hope it's still unlocked," Lizzie said, crossing her fingers. She pushed open the door. *"Vamos."* She grinned and stood aside as Gael and Paloma entered. The garden was dimly lit. It took a few seconds for Paloma's eyes to adjust, but soon she could see the outline of the trees, large leafy plants, and lilies that covered Frida's courtyard.

"What's the plan?" Paloma asked.

"I'll hide here to make sure no one comes. If anyone shows up, like a security guard, I'll whistle like a bird. Gael knows my whistle. Stay low so the security cameras in the trees don't capture your face."

Paloma trembled at the thought of a security guard or police officer catching them. She wished she could be brave like Lulu Pennywhistle, but a chill shot up her back. Gael must have sensed it, because he gave her arm a gentle squeeze.

"It'll be okay," he said. "Lizzie will keep watch while we check out the room and become heroes."

Lizzie snapped at Gael in Spanish, causing him to lower his head like a punished child.

"I'm not going to waste our time," he answered back in English to her.

"Keep it simple," she whispered to both of them. "Get into the room. Find out what's in there. Make it quick. Don't use this until you're at the door." Lizzie handed a small flashlight to Gael. "*Buena suerte. Good luck!*"

Gael and Paloma sped through the garden, past the gift shop, and around the cafeteria to the tree they had discovered the day before. As they squeezed between the tree branches toward the door, Paloma couldn't believe what she saw.

The door was already open! Light glowed from inside the room and spilled into the darkness. Paloma looked over at Gael. "What do we do now?" she mouthed to him.

Gael put a finger over his lips. Paloma nodded in understanding. Although her heart felt like it'd jump out of her chest, she wasn't about to make a noise. Gael stepped closer to the open door. He stopped when the tree rustled and sent a spray of leaves crashing against the ground. Paloma wiped her palms against her jeans.

Gael grabbed the doorknob and peeked into the room.

Every hair on Paloma's body felt like it was standing up. She prayed no one was inside. Gael nodded to her and waved her over. Paloma felt suddenly woozy, but somehow she managed to move one foot in front of the other and follow Gael into the room. The golden glow from a lightbulb that dangled from the ceiling revealed a room crowded with ladders, metal paint buckets, a wheelbarrow, and a couple of wheelchairs partially covered with blankets.

Paloma exhaled. "It's just a storage room," she whispered.

Gael beamed his flashlight toward a dark corner of the room. "That's why it was unlocked," he said, his voice oozing disappointment. "There's probably a janitor here tonight. We should leave before he comes back."

"What's that?" Paloma said, taking Gael's flashlight to point at the ground near a wheelchair. A flicker of gold blinked in the flashlight's beam.

She picked it up. "It's a Mexican peso, I think," Paloma said, showing Gael. "Except it has this weird little knobby thing attached to it."

"That's a cuff link," Gael whispered. He tossed the cuff link between his two hands. "It's heavy. Real gold. Men wear them with their suits." He handed the cuff link back to Paloma.

"Do janitors wear them?" Paloma asked, already knowing the answer to the question.

"Not the janitors I know—"

Lizzie's whistle was distant, but it shot through the

garden, the rustling tree behind them, and straight through Paloma's chest like an arrow. Someone was coming. She quickly buried the cuff link in her back jean pocket.

Paloma felt frozen until Gael clutched her hand. "Let's go!" They rushed out the door, but before they could duck out of sight, they heard steps approaching.

Their only exit was blocked. Gael gazed up toward the tree branches like he wanted to climb.

"Don't even think about it!" Paloma whispered, and pulled him back into the janitorial closet. She grabbed one of the dusty blankets from atop a wheelchair, and gestured for Gael to squat under an old wooden desk. She quickly spread the blanket over the desk and snuck beneath it just as the door gave out a long whine.

Someone walked into the room. From a ripped hole in the blanket, Paloma saw a man's shiny black dress shoes and black pants. A flashlight blazed across the room. Paloma and Gael huddled together. Paloma wondered if this mystery man was looking for the cuff link. Was it his? She peeked out again. Gael tapped her arm and shook his head for her to stop. She didn't care; she had to see who it was. She wanted a glimpse of his face, but all she got was the back of a long black trench coat. The man stepped carefully across the room. Paloma noticed his limp. With every uneven step he took, Paloma's heart pounded in her chest. Who was this guy? What was he doing there? What would he do if he found them? The man lifted the wheelbarrow across from them and dropped it back down.

Suddenly, he started speaking Spanish, as if he knew they were there. Paloma shrunk back in fear, and Gael's eyes widened. Paloma caught a few words but not enough to understand what was happening. Gael gave her a frightened look and gestured for her to remain quiet.

Just then, something brushed against Paloma's neck. She swiped at it, hoping it wasn't a spider. Gael looked at her with a warning stare to stop squirming, but she couldn't help it. The creepy crawly sensation continued. It was definitely a spider!

Paloma swiped frantically at her neck, accidently sending the spider flying toward Gael's face. He let out a surprised yelp. There was a terrible moment of complete silence as Gael clapped a hand over his mouth. But then feet stomped toward their hiding spot—and Paloma felt the Trench Coat Man's hands clamp down on her ankles.

Chapter 14

The Trench Coat Man

Paloma screamed and squirmed as he dragged her out from under the desk. Gael kept ahold of her hands, pulling her back under the desk. Paloma felt like the rope in a game of tug-of-war. Suddenly, when the Trench Coat Man got a good look at Paloma, he looked confused, and his grasp on her ankles slacked. It was just enough of a pause for Paloma to smash her foot against his chin. It landed. The man fell back, losing his balance. But soon he easily recovered and grasped her ankle again.

"*¿Quién—*" he started to say to Paloma, when a second shadowy figure barged into the room and slammed something sturdy against the side of the Trench Coat Man's head. He collapsed to the floor with a groan.

"*¡Vámanos!*" Lizzie yelled as she strapped on her trumpet case and pulled Paloma up onto her feet. Lizzie and Gael took Paloma under their arms and rushed her back through the patio and out of the museum door they had entered. "*Estás bien*, Paloma," Lizzie whispered. "Breathe."

Tears poured from Paloma's eyes. She couldn't believe what had just happened. Lizzie and Gael were half carrying her down Allende Street. The air around her suddenly felt thick, like she was trying to breathe through a heavy blanket. Paloma tried to stop Lizzie and Gael by putting her feet down firmly on the sidewalk, but they lifted her and kept moving.

"We have to get farther away," Lizzie whispered. "We can't stop yet, Paloma."

"I need air," she gasped. She didn't know where they were, but Lizzie and Gael finally stopped behind some bushes. Paloma plopped down on the wet ground and tried to catch her breath. Lizzie crouched over her, rubbing Paloma's back.

"You're okay, Kansas," Lizzie whispered, and flicked on her flashlight to check Paloma's ankle for any injury. "You're fine. Try to relax."

After a few seconds, Paloma felt better. "I thought he was going to hurt us." Paloma's voice broke as she fought back the urge to cry.

Gael sunk down next to Paloma and took over rubbing Paloma's back while Lizzie stood guard over them both.

"Lizzie hit him hard with her trumpet case," Gael said. "Like I said, never make a mariachi mad."

"It's not funny, *hermano*," Lizzie said.

"You're tough, too, Paloma," Gael said. "You fought back."

Paloma gave him a faint smile. She didn't feel tough. Right now, she felt exhausted and confused.

"That guy was definitely *not* a janitor," Paloma said. She rubbed her ankles. Both were a bit tender, but there were no bruises. "Who was he? He spoke Spanish, but it sounded weird."

"He spoke to you?" Lizzie asked. "What did he say?"

"He said he knew we were there," Gael answered.

"He also said something . . ." Paloma said. "Something about the *anillo*. I know I heard that word."

Gael started shaking his head. "He never said *anillo*."

"My Spanish is bad, but I know I heard it," Paloma said, frustrated that Gael was denying it. Of everything the man said, the one thing she caught was the Spanish word for "ring." Did she hear him wrong?

"Doesn't matter," Lizzie said, and gave Gael a concerned look. "I saw him limping across the courtyard, and that's why I whistled. He came out of nowhere, as if he'd been at the museum the whole time. He probably saw you guys in the courtyard."

"We heard your whistle, but it was too late," Paloma said. "We had to hide."

"Maybe he's the one who opened the secret room before we—" Gael started. Lizzie interrupted him with a raised finger.

"I hear something," Lizzie whispered as she stole a look over the bushes and scanned the area. She took a few steps and hid behind a nearby tree, peering toward the museum. Gael and Paloma held their breaths. First, they heard only the bristling of the night wind, but from the wind emerged the hum of a car slowing down. Lizzie raced back behind the bushes and hunched down next to Paloma. "Stay down. A car is coming."

After a few seconds, a black car slowly approached, and stopped in the middle of the street. The click of the car door opening sent a chill straight up Paloma's spine. She wanted nothing more than to get out of there. Gael, again sensing her anxiety, held her hand. Paloma peeked through the shrubs and saw the man in the black trench coat get out of the car and walk out of sight. Soon the only sound in the night was the steady *step, drag, step* of his unbalanced footsteps against the sidewalk. *Step. Drag. Step. Step. Drag. Step.* Paloma's ankle suddenly throbbed in pain again.

The driver remained in the car. Paloma strained to see who it was, but all she could see was a dark shadow. The Trench Coat Man returned to the car, and as he got in, he massaged the side of his head that Lizzie slammed with her trumpet case and spouted an angry jumble of hissing words that sounded like "shoe," "mushroom," "shush," and "shrek." Paloma recognized it instantly. It was the same language she heard the Fortune-Teller speaking earlier to some tourists. The car drove off.

"We're not safe here. We have to go," Lizzie said as soon as the car was out of sight. She yanked Paloma up from the ground. The three of them bolted down Allende to Paris Street and didn't stop running until they arrived at Paloma's house. Lizzie grabbed the key from Paloma's trembling hand and opened the gate. They scrambled up the wet tree to her room. Once inside, Paloma and Gael sat cross-legged on her bed while Lizzie remained near the windowsill to keep a lookout.

"Do you think the Trench Coat Man followed us?" Paloma asked.

"*No sé.*" Lizzie shrugged. "Whoever he is, hopefully he gave up."

"What language was he speaking? Was it French or German? Did you catch it?" Gael asked.

Paloma nodded. "I think it was Russian."

"It was definitely Russian," Lizzie said. She gave Gael a serious look. "Something big is going on, Gael. Bigger than we thought."

Gael's eyes widened.

"What do you mean, bigger than you thought?" Paloma asked.

Lizzie looked out the window, and Gael shifted uncomfortably on the bed.

"What's going on, you guys?" Paloma said, frustrated. They weren't telling her everything. "What would Russians want at Frida's house? Why would that guy be in the mop room? He was searching for something just like we were. He definitely said something about a ring."

"If he's looking for the ring, too . . ." Lizzie said, gazing at her brother. Her shoulders slumped. "We have to find it before he does."

"We will," Paloma said, when without warning her bedroom door burst open. Her mom stood at the doorway in her robe and slippers.

"Paloma Jane Marquez! Where have you been?" she yelled. "I woke up and found your bed empty. Empty!" She collapsed at the edge of the bed and covered her face with her hands. "I thought you'd been kidnapped or something," she sobbed, wiping her nose with a Kleenex she pulled from her robe pocket. "Where were you?"

"I'm sorry," Paloma said, taking her mom's hands. "I can explain."

"Can you?" her mother shouted, and then pulled Paloma into an embrace. "I'm so mad at you right now. I was just in the dining room, calling Professor Breton for help and waiting for a horrible phone call from the police. Another horrible phone call, Paloma!"

Paloma knew about the horrible phone call. Her mom had received one nine years ago while waiting for Paloma's dad to come home. Paloma could feel her mom's heart banging against her chest, and hugged her tight. She hated to see her mom cry. She hated more that she was the reason.

"I'm here, Mom," Paloma said through tears. "I'm sorry I scared you."

Paloma's mom broke the embrace and stood up. "You two are no longer welcome in our home."

"Mom!" Paloma protested. Gael and Lizzie both lowered their heads. "It's my fault, not theirs! I wanted churros."

"I don't care!" Paloma's mom said, throwing her hands up. "I trusted all three of you, and now I know I can't."

"*Lo siento,* Señora Marquez," Lizzie said.

"Sorry," Gael repeated. "We didn't mean to worry you. We were just hanging out—"

"Señora Marquez—" Lizzie said.

"Well, I hope it was worth it, because it's the last time you'll get to hang out," Paloma's mom said.

"Señora Marquez—" Lizzie tried again.

"I'll be calling your parents tomorrow."

"Señora Marquez, there is a man standing at the gate," Lizzie said with an urgency that snapped Paloma's mom to attention. Lizzie's eyes were transfixed on something outside.

"What? Is it Professor Breton?" Paloma's mom asked as she rushed to the windowsill. She peered outside and gasped.

Gael and Paloma lurched forward to see. Paloma hoped it was Professor Breton coming over to help her mom, but the hair standing up on the back of her neck told her it wasn't. The man in the black trench coat stood motionless in front of their gate.

"That's not Professor Breton. Who is that?" Paloma's mom asked.

Paloma had a quick second of panic. Had they closed the gate all the way when they came through?

"He's trying to open the gate," Lizzie said with panic. The man pushed up against the gate with his body and then jiggled the gate handle.

"Who is this guy?" Paloma's mom asked again. Terrified, Paloma grabbed for her mom's hand to pull her away from the window. Gael glanced at her in a way that meant he, too, knew it was the Trench Coat Man.

"How long has he been there?" Paloma's mom asked.

"He just showed up," Lizzie answered.

"Did this man follow you?" The three kids shrugged. "I'm calling the po—"

Suddenly, a black car pulled up. The kids watched the familiar *step, drag, step . . . step, drag, step* of the man's walk before he got into the car, and it drove off into the night.

Chapter 15

Keeping a Secret

Paloma grabbed a seat at the back of the classroom and pulled out her note cards. She was the first to arrive at her Mexican art and culture class. An entire day had passed since her mom had busted her for sneaking out with Gael and Lizzie. She spent the whole day at home apologizing to her mom and obsessing over the Trench Coat Man. She wanted so badly to talk to Gael and Lizzie, but her mom had taken her phone away. She forbade Paloma from seeing the Castillos for the rest of their time in Coyoacán. She even threatened to call the university tutoring program, or worse . . . their parents. It was the most upset Paloma had ever seen her mom.

Still, it wasn't going to stop Paloma from finding the

peacock ring. She was more determined than ever. The fact that the Trench Coat Man had been in the locked room at midnight proved to her that they were on the right track. Paloma pulled out the note card with her observations.

Trench Coat Man

Black trench coat, dark hair, pale, tall, strong, walks with a limp, speaks Russian, speaks Spanish, searching for something in the locked room, too. He knows where I live in Coyoacán.

The last thought chilled Paloma. Was she in danger? Had she put her mom in danger, too? Her mind raced back to that night, grasping for any memories that would help her figure out what was really going on.

Paloma's pen raced across the note card, adding her thoughts.

He looked at me like he wasn't expecting to see me. When he said in Spanish that he knew "we" were there, who was he really expecting to find in the locked room?

Soon, a bunch of people of all ages streamed into the classroom. Everyone spoke English, but a few had accents from different European countries. She'd never been in a class with adults and teenagers before, let alone Europeans. Paloma shuffled her note cards and gave the newcomers a shy smile as they took seats around her and greeted her.

"Welcome to Introduction to Mexican Art and Culture!" sang a voice Paloma recognized. It was Professor Breton. He strolled into the classroom, opened his laptop at the front of the room, and sat at the edge of his desk facing the students.

"*¡Bienvenidos a todos!*" he said, giving Paloma a special wink. "The objective of this four-week course is to expose you to the vibrant culture, art, and traditions of Mexico. Of course, we cannot cover all of Mexico's diverse culture in four weeks. That, my friends, is impossible! This class should be considered simply a shoreline to get your feet wet. Once you're through here, it's up to you to fully dive in!"

Although Paloma felt out of place as the youngest in the classroom, knowing that Professor Breton was the teacher made her feel better. After all, two nights ago when he'd arrived at the Marquez's home, he'd calmed her mother down and taken Gael and Lizzie home. Perhaps Professor Breton could be a valuable ally to her.

Professor Breton stood at the front of the class and clicked through a slide show displaying Mexican cultural traditions and art. When he stopped on an image of Frida Kahlo, Paloma sat up straight. It was a self-portrait she'd never seen. In this painting, Frida was seated, wearing a white blouse. Two parrots sat on her lap, while two others perched on her shoulders. On Frida's fingers were several rings.

"This is the artist Frida Kahlo," Professor Breton said. "Many of you probably have heard of her and have most likely already visited her home, Casa Azul, here in Coyoacán, correct?" Paloma looked around the room. A few students nodded.

"Professor, what's up with Frida and the overgrown eyebrows?" asked a teenage girl with an American accent. "Didn't she believe in waxing?" The entire classroom laughed, and Paloma couldn't help but chuckle, too. When she had first seen the poster of Frida at the airport, she had also joked that Frida needed a salon appointment. Now Paloma saw things differently. The laughter subsided, and Paloma raised her hand.

Professor Breton nodded toward her.

"When I first saw one of her self-portraits, I thought the same thing," Paloma said. "Then I learned how painting saved Frida's life. It was freedom to her. She didn't paint what society expected her to paint. She painted what she felt. Now that I know more about Frida, I don't see the hairy eyebrows anymore. I see a perfect bird with its wings expanded in flight. I think it represents her soul soaring."

The classroom was silent. Paloma felt the attention of the entire classroom. Could they see what she saw?

"That's super deep," the girl said, glancing away from the self-portrait on the screen to smile at Paloma. "Are you sure you're not the world's youngest art professor?"

Paloma blushed. She thought she'd pass out from embarrassment right there on the spot.

"Well said, Paloma," Professor Breton said. "And I can add that Frida was one of the few celebrated female artists at a time when Picasso, Matisse, and her husband, Diego Rivera, were getting all the attention of the art world. She's so important that the Mexican government decreed all of Frida Kahlo's work to be a national patrimony."

"What's that?" Paloma asked.

"It means her work, her art, and her personal items are protected by Mexico and cannot be taken outside of the country without special permissions. Permissions that are rarely granted."

Paloma scrambled to grab her note cards to write everything Professor Breton said and ended up sending several note cards sailing across the classroom floor. She collected them and took a deep breath. She needed to get a grip! Did Gael and Lizzie know about Frida's work being protected by Mexico?

During a break, Paloma walked with the other students to a small stand outside the front of the school to buy a juice. She was sitting on a stone bench alone sipping orange juice and reading through her note cards when someone called her name. Gael peeked out from behind some trees.

"Is it safe?"

Paloma looked around for any signs of Professor Breton. "Safe!" She was so happy to see her friend, she hugged him. "How'd you find me?"

"I called you yesterday, but your mom says she took your phone away," Gael said, and frowned. "Lizzie and I feel really bad about that."

"It's okay." Paloma shrugged. "My mom will eventually cave in and give it back to me. She never stays angry long."

"I wanted to make sure you were fine. I followed you and your mom on a bus from your house. When you jumped off, I jumped off, too. I've been waiting for you to come out. What's going on? Why are you here in this academic puppet factory?" Gael lifted his arms like he was a marionette being pulled by strings.

"You definitely talk like an artist." Paloma giggled. "I told you my mom enrolled me in some summer classes. She wants me to be occupied with productive endeavors and embrace opportunities!" she said in her best professor voice. "So here I am embracing stuff. After this class, I have Beginner's Spanish."

"That's horrible," Gael said, wincing. "They're going to teach you things like '*Hola, amigo. ¿Cómo estás tú?*' You're better than that."

"No, I'm not, but thanks! Are you and Lizzie okay? Has my mom called your parents yet?"

"Not yet. I hope she doesn't. My dad's super busy in New York, and my mom is worried about him because he's so far away. She doesn't need any more stress."

"Well, I'm glad you're here." Paloma smiled. "I learned in class that Frida's artwork was decreed as a national patrimony by the Mexican government. That's an important detail, don't you think?"

"I knew that," Gael said with a slight shrug. "It's cool, right?"

Paloma bit down on her bottom lip, annoyed that once again Gael held back valuable information about Frida from her. "What? Why didn't you tell me?"

"I didn't think it mattered," Gael said. "Sorry."

"Just like you didn't think Frida's urn mattered? Of course it matters! When solving cases, Lulu always has to understand motives. Why do people do things? These important details could help us find the ring." Paloma's mind raced with theories. "If her work and jewelry are protected, it makes it much more valuable. Maybe the Trench Coat Man is planning to take the ring outside of Mexico. The Mexican government needs to be informed. We have to tell them."

"They won't believe a bunch of kids," Gael said. "They'll laugh in our faces."

"Can we call your dad for more information? You said he was talking to a friend on the phone when you overheard him mention the peacock ring. Could we speak to his friend?"

"Impossible," Gael said. "We don't know who the friend was, and we barely speak to our dad since he's been in New York. We only talk to him every other week. He's super busy."

"But doesn't the Trench Coat Man change things? If he finds the ring before we do, it will be lost for good. We can't let that happen."

Gael pulled on his eagle warrior medallion and shuffled his feet uncomfortably. "You're right, but we can't speak to my dad about this," Gael said. "It won't help anything."

Paloma stared at him coolly. Something wasn't right. Frustrated, she turned away from him and watched the last few students head back inside the school. It was strangely quiet outside now.

"Oh, sweet Frida! I'm late for class!" Paloma shot up and grabbed her bag and juice. "I gotta go! If I mess up anymore, my mom will send me back to Kansas. Seriously! She was looking at flights last night."

Gael kept pace with her as she rushed back to the school entrance. "I'm sorry we got you in trouble with your mom."

"I'll survive. Look, the main thing is we're closing in on the ring and we have to keep going, but we need to be able to communicate. There's a planter in front of my gate. You know it, right?"

Gael nodded.

"We can leave messages for each other under the leaves of the plant until I get my phone back. We can't let Trench Coat Man find the peacock ring. Nobody grabs my ankles, steals from Frida, and gets away with it!"

"Suena bien," Gael said as Paloma rushed into the school.

Once the door closed behind her, Paloma stopped to

watch Gael walk away. Her heart thumped hard in her chest. Why was he against asking his dad for more information? And how did he not know who his dad's friend was? She didn't want to admit it, but deep down she knew Gael was keeping something from her. But what? And why?

Chapter 16

The Black Car

The next morning before class, Paloma found a note from Gael in the planter in front of their house. While her mom locked the gate, Paloma tucked it into her bag to read later in class. From the corner of her eye, Paloma saw a black car parked a few houses down. She had never noticed it parked on her block before. Was it the same car that followed them from Casa Azul? Was she being paranoid? Paloma squatted down like she was tying her shoes to get a better look at its license plate, but there was none, which she thought was strange. Didn't all cars have to use license plates? Maybe Mexico had different rules . . .

As Paloma walked with her mom to the bus stop, she made a point of watching passing cars and checked for license plates. All of them had one. She had to warn Gael and Lizzie. Maybe there was a car outside their house watching them, too?

Once she was seated in class, Paloma opened Gael's note. On the note card, he had sketched Frida Kahlo with her arms crossed over her chest and a pout on her face. Above it was a bubble with the words *"¿Donde está mi anillo?"* Paloma giggled out loud. She envied Gael's mad sketching skills. Next to the sketch was a scribbled note, "We saw a black car parked on our street last night. Be careful. We are being watched."

All through Beginner's Spanish, Paloma thought about the black car. She was relieved when class ended, but she couldn't let on to Professor Breton, who had promised to drop her off at home.

"Your mom has invited us to lunch at Pepe Coyotes today," he said, opening his car door for Paloma.

"Good, I'm starving," Paloma said. "I could eat a million tacos!"

"Well, then I'm glad she's paying."

Paloma giggled. "Isn't that near the Jardín Centenario?"

"That's right. You know your way around already?"

Once they arrived at the park, Professor Breton found parking a few blocks away from Pepe Coyotes. As they walked toward the restaurant, Paloma spotted the Fortune-Teller packing up her jewelry into a bag.

"Do you mind if I look at her rings real fast?"

Professor Breton looked at his watch. "Sure, we're early. I'll call your mom to let her know we're close." Paloma walked up to the Fortune-Teller, curious about where she was going.

"Slow day for jewelry?" Paloma asked, sneaking up behind the Fortune-Teller as she hoisted a bag full of her wares.

"Very slow," the woman answered with a faint smile. "I'm going to go to the *mercado* to try to find better luck. I've been looking for the peacock ring that you asked for . . ."

Paloma froze. She had forgotten that she had opened her big mouth about the peacock ring.

"Sadly, I cannot find one like that. Is there another ring you'd like?"

"It's okay. Thanks for looking," Paloma said. She glanced over by the churro stand and tugged on her medallion. Neither Gael nor Lizzie was there.

"You wear an eagle warrior around your neck. Did the boy with the black hat give it to you?"

"How did you know?"

"He bought two of them from me, and now he only wears one," she answered. "I notice these things because he was one of my first customers. He told his sister that they were going to need protection. He bought the Aztec warriors. She bought a gold crucifix. I gave them a good price because I could tell they were desperate."

Paloma stepped back, confused. "Desperate? About what?" she asked.

"Something about their father . . . Yes, he was going away."

Paloma got goosebumps. Why did they buy medallions to protect themselves? What did they need protecting from? When Paloma had first told Gael that she was suspicious of the Fortune-Teller, he hadn't mentioned that he bought the medallions from her.

"You should tell them to be careful. You should be careful, too. And I should be going," the Fortune-Teller said matter-of-factly. *"Hasta luego."*

"What?" Paloma was stunned. As the Fortune-Teller strolled away, a postcard fell from her bag. Paloma rushed to swoop it up and noticed Professor Breton approaching. She almost called out to the Fortune-Teller but thought better of it once she glanced over the postcard. It wasn't a postcard at all. Professor Breton stepped next to Paloma.

"Hey, that's an invitation to Frida's birthday party. How did a fortune-teller get invited to the party of the year?" he quipped. "Come on, we're late now."

At the restaurant, Paloma's mom placed a plate of chicken tacos in front of her. Paloma spooned salsa over them and replayed in her head the conversation she had with the Fortune-Teller. Why were Gael and Lizzie desperate? Just because their dad was in New York City? It didn't make sense.

"Your daughter is looking for a peacock ring," Professor

Breton blurted, causing Paloma to snap out of her thoughts. She rolled her eyes at him.

"What?" He put his hands up in surrender. "I'm sorry, but I thought that's what the Fortune-Teller said. She said you wanted a peacock ring, no? I'm sorry. Did I ruin a surprise?"

"Oh, Paloma. Not the rings again," her mom said, shaking her head. "Since when did you get so into jewelry? It's because your twelve now, right? I read about this. Today it's jewelry. Tomorrow it'll be eyeliner and lipstick. I swear I'm not ready for any of it."

Professor Breton shot her mom a sympathetic look. Paloma took a bite of her chicken taco and watched her mom get worked up. She wanted to tell her that lipstick and eyeliner were the last thing she needed to worry about, but she stayed quiet and swallowed another bite of taco. She had to admit, mystery-solving made her hungry.

"Well, if you don't buy her a peacock ring, I'd be happy to buy you one, Paloma. You've been an absolute delight to have in my class these past two days."

"She has?" Paloma's mom dropped her taco on her plate.

"Why do you say it like that, Mom?" Paloma asked with a sour face. "His class is actually not boring."

"Thank you, Paloma." Professor Breton grinned. "You should have seen her in action yesterday. She could have taught a whole course on Frida Kahlo. The other students were in awe. Today, all of them were asking her more about Frida. She's learned a lot in just the short time she's been here."

"Really?" Paloma's mom sat back and wiped her mouth with a napkin.

"Why is that so hard to believe?" Paloma asked. "I told you I've been doing productive things and embracing stuff. I've been learning all about Frida Kahlo, one of Mexico's most controversial and talented artists, but all you see is the one night I snuck out for churros."

"Well, that was enough!" Paloma's mom said, dropping her napkin on the table in a dramatic flurry. "I thought I had lost my daughter that night."

Paloma sheepishly lowered her head and waited for her mom to take a swig from her bottled water. Scaring her mom filled Paloma with regret, but she knew she'd do it again if it meant catching the Trench Coat Man and finding the peacock ring.

Later that evening, Paloma's thoughts swirled. When she got home that afternoon, the black car was no longer there. Relieved, she headed straight for her room, sprawled out on her bed, and took out the invitation the Fortune-Teller had dropped and a blank note card. She wrote down everything she knew about the Fortune-Teller.

Fortune-Teller

Clear gray eyes. Dark hair. Speaks Russian. Arrived two weeks ago. Tells fortunes with stones. Sells jewelry. Special rings for serious buyers. Knows Gael and Lizzie. Sold them medallions. Knows I'm looking for a peacock ring. Invited to Frida's birthday party.

Could the Fortune-Teller be involved somehow? Paloma wasn't so sure. Now there were new players in the arena: the Trench Coat Man and whoever was in the black car watching them. Someone had been in the driver's seat the other night. Who was it? Paloma wrote up another note card and titled it "Black Car."

Exhausted from thinking so much, Paloma tucked the card in her bag with the others. Before she went to bed, she wrote Gael a note asking him to meet her during school break. Then, just as her head hit the pillow, Paloma heard the soft hum of a car engine outside. She stooped low, crawled to her window, and peered out. The black car was back.

Chapter 17

I See You!

As her mom locked the gate behind them the next morning, Paloma spotted the black car parked curbside between two other cars. She moved toward the planter, left her note for Gael, and remained there, pretending to check the plant for bad leaves as she squinted toward the car. She wished she had a pair of binoculars or super-vision powers to see if anyone was inside. Was it the Trench Coat Man? Or was it his driver from the other night? Suddenly, the car pulled out and drove off.

"What are you doing, Paloma?" Her mom had just noticed that Paloma was clutching a bunch of leaves in her hands. "You're going to kill that plant."

"Just a little light pruning." Paloma smiled and dropped the leaves.

"*Vamos*, little bird. We're late," she said. "Are you enjoying your classes? Or has it been like watching people floss?" her mom asked as they walked down the street.

Paloma giggled. "It's not so bad. Professor Breton makes it fun. I think he keeps adding more Frida into the class just for me."

Her mom chuckled. "He's a good guy," she said. "Has he shown you the painting of Frida's dress hanging in front of a New York City background yet?"

Paloma shook head. Her mom signaled for the oncoming bus to stop for them, and they got on.

"No," Paloma said. "Why?"

"It was your dad's favorite Frida Kahlo painting." Paloma took out a note card from her bag as soon as they found seats on the bus. "Speaking of Frida Kahlo . . ." her mom started. "We told the Farills that we'd go see the art exhibit in Mexico City with them, but I can't go. I'm seriously behind on my paper."

"Whoa! I forgot all about it," Paloma said. "I really wanted to go because there's supposed to be some Frida art."

"Well, I called Mrs. Farill last night, and she said they're still going despite everything that's happened."

"What do you mean? What happened?"

"Apparently, someone broke into their house this week,"

Paloma's mom said. "Luckily, no one was home and nothing valuable was taken, but the family is shaken."

"Poor Tavo," Paloma said. "What about the dogs?"

"Everyone was fine. House was empty. Anyway, that's all I know. You can ask Tavo more about it when you see him this weekend."

"So I can go?"

"If you're okay going without me. Professor Breton says that I should encourage your interest in art. He says that you're a natural." Paloma's mom nudged her playfully.

Paloma chuckled. Professor Breton thought she was a natural. She liked how that sounded and couldn't help but repeat the word with a big grin on her face. "A natural," she said.

"I mean, it's the Farills. They're lovely people and you get along well with Tavo, right?"

"Yep!" Paloma leaned in to give her mom a kiss on the cheek. "Can I have my phone back to call Tavo and confirm when they'll pick me up?"

"Nice try." She smirked at Paloma. "I'll call Mrs. Farill and make the arrangements."

In class, Paloma made a point to ask Professor Breton about the painting her mom mentioned was her father's favorite. He quickly pulled it up on his laptop for the entire classroom.

"It's on display at Casa Azul, if you want to see the real

thing," Professor Breton said. She made a mental note to view it the next time she was there.

At break, Paloma had hoped that Gael and Lizzie would show up, but break time came and went, and there was no sign of them. Paloma wished she could talk to them. She couldn't stop thinking about what the Fortune-Teller had told her about them wanting protection when their dad left for New York. Paloma knew how it felt to be without a dad, but this was different. Their dad was on a trip to New York. It wasn't like he'd be gone forever. Why would they be so concerned about protection? Paloma flashed back to when Gael had given her the medallion and told her it would protect her.

Paloma could barely focus in Spanish class. When the teacher asked her in Spanish what she planned to be when she grew up, Paloma answered, *"Papas fritas,"* French fries.

After class, Professor Breton dropped Paloma off at home. Once he was out of sight, she rushed to the planter. Her note to Gael was gone, but he hadn't left one for her.

Paloma frowned with disappointment. She looked down the block, and once again, the black car was sitting there. She felt like rushing it, pounding the window with her fists, and demanding answers. The only thing that kept her from attacking the car was the fact that she wasn't ready for another rumble with the Trench Coat Man. Not without Lizzie and her trumpet case close by.

Later that night, Paloma did the next best thing she could think of. After all, Lulu Pennywhistle never let anyone intimidate her. Paloma grabbed a note card and drew a picture of the black car. It wasn't as nice a sketch as Gael would have done, but it would get the message across. Above it, Paloma wrote, "I see you!"

The black car was still there. She waved the note card in the air and then buried it in the planter. She felt bold. She felt very Lulu-ish and also a bit Frida-ish.

"Come and get it," she said.

Chapter 18

Self-Portrait with a Braid

For the trip to the musem, Paloma dressed in her favorite red skinny jeans, a black concert T-shirt, and a long black cardigan sweater. Paloma fixed her hair into a side braid and topped off her outfit with the eagle warrior medallion.

She found her mom downstairs humming a song in the kitchen, so she raced outside to the planter to see if her "I see you" note was still there. It was gone. The black car was gone, too. She went inside the house feeling victorious. Maybe they got the message and left once and for all.

She grabbed her mom from behind and gave her a hug.

"That's nice, little bird. I haven't had a hug from you in a long time," her mom said, spinning around to drop a kiss on Paloma's forehead. "You've got your spending money from your grandparents?"

Paloma patted her bag. "It's all here," she said.

"Good! Don't go crazy spending all your pesos at once. We still have three weeks here."

"I won't." Paloma smiled. "Are you working on your paper all day?"

"Yes, I'll be at the university, and then Professor Breton will bring me home. I thought we could all have dinner together so you can tell us about your day. Sound good?"

Paloma nodded just as the bell from the gate rang. Tavo and his parents were right on time. Her mom walked her out to Tavo, who was wearing a Diego Rivera T-shirt.

"You look awesome," Tavo said, pulling his sunglasses off. "Are you ready to have your mind blown by more Mexican art today?"

"*¡Por supuesto!*" Paloma chuckled, squeezing into the back seat of the white Range Rover. From the front, Tavo's parents turned to welcome her. In return, Paloma wanted to say how sorry she was to hear that their home had been broken into, but she kept quiet. Maybe this excursion was their way of forgetting all about it.

The ride to Museo Soumaya was only a twenty-minute drive. From the outside, the museum looked like a shiny aluminum trophy that had been run over by a truck. Paloma had never seen a museum like it. She and Tavo took a dozen selfies in front of it.

Once inside, Tavo and Paloma rushed up the white floors to the fourth level to see artwork by Mexico's finest artists. The two passed paintings by artists named Orozco, Siqueiros, and Tamayo before pausing at Frida Kahlo's *Self-Portrait with Braid*. In the portrait, Frida's dark hair was tied up into braids and knots at the top of her head. A dark red ribbon weaved through her hair. Around her neck was a necklace made of stones. Her shoulders were bare and covered only by large green leaves.

"This one is different," Paloma said, studying the painting. "It's different from her other self-portraits."

"How so, *querida*?" Mr. Farill said, suddenly standing next to her and Tavo.

"Well, because . . ." Paloma started. She gave the painting a long gaze, absorbing every detail. "In her other self-portraits, Frida has her hair down or up, but in this painting her hair is pulled tight and twisted into knots at the top of her head."

"Very good. Go on. What else?" Mr. Farill said.

"Seriously, Dad?" Tavo said, rolling his eyes. "This isn't art class."

Paloma giggled but continued. "Frida uses lots of background images in her self-portraits, like birds, butterflies, trees, and even clouds, but this one is pretty bare. In this one, she chose an ugly green-yellow color behind her. There's not much else. Also, her shoulders are uncovered. In most of her paintings, she has a blouse or shawl on. I'm not sure why she did it this way."

Mr. Farill stood silently, rubbing his chin. "You could be an art professor, Miss Paloma," he said finally. "Or a detective. You have a keen eye." He smiled at her. "If you want to know why she painted this one differently, there is another clue, but it's not in the painting. It's revealed in the year this painting was made by Frida. Sometimes timing is everything." He pointed over at the title tag on the wall beside the painting.

Tavo read it out loud. "*Self-Portrait with a Braid.* 1941. Frida Kahlo."

"This painting was done the year after Frida remarried Diego Rivera," Mr. Farill explained. "See, Frida was a deliberate painter. Every color and image meant something to her. At this time in her life, she painted her hair knotted up in braids atop her head. Many believe it had to do with the fact that she was confused about whether she had made the right choice to remarry Diego."

Paloma thought about how her stomach had felt tied up in knots after she spoke to the Fortune-Teller about Gael and Lizzie. Everything the Fortune-Teller said about her friends being desperate and buying medallions for protection confused her.

"And what does that necklace symbolize?" Paloma asked.

"This is the same necklace she wore the day they remarried in San Francisco. It's made from rare pre-Columbian stones. That is what is so intriguing about her self-portraits. She is giving you clues into her life."

Paloma eyed the painting. "Where is the necklace now?" she asked. "Is it on display somewhere I can see it?"

"Most of it is on display at her museum," Mr. Farill answered. "Although two weeks ago, a man who assisted with one of the exhibits at Casa Azul was arrested for stealing several pieces belonging to the museum. He's in jail now."

Paloma flashed him an are-you-serious? look. "Did they get the jewelry back?" she asked.

Mr. Farill shook his head. "They only retrieved a jade necklace. What he did with the other pieces, we may never know. It's all very tragic for Mexico to lose these valuable pieces."

Paloma stood there in a daze. Did Gael and Lizzie know about this? Was the peacock ring one of the stolen items?

"Now they're finally putting security cameras inside the museum," Tavo said. "A little too late."

Mr. Farill shook his head angrily. "It's disgusting," he hissed.

Paloma looked to Tavo for an explanation.

"My dad thinks that putting cameras inside Frida's museum destroys the dignity of her childhood home. He was against it. It was a big fight, but the museum went ahead and started installing cameras everywhere."

"Those security cameras don't do anything anyway. I mean we have them in our home, and it was still broken into. Why ruin the spirit of Frida's home with vulgar technology that doesn't work?" He shook his head with disgust.

"My mom told me about what happened. I'm so sorry," Paloma said, touching the coolness of her eagle warrior medallion between her fingers. "I'm glad no one was hurt."

"Thank you. You're sweet," Mr. Farill said. "We've got the culprits on film. We'll catch them. Anyway, as I was saying, Frida's home is a historical site. It's shameful to put up security cameras in every corner."

Paloma tried her best to follow everything Tavo and his father were saying, but her mind kept zooming in on the missing jewelry at Casa Azul.

"Mr. Farill, do they know what other pieces were stolen from the museum? Was there a ring?"

Mr. Farill leaned back in surprise. "Yes, there was a ring of some importance . . ." Mr. Farill rubbed his chin. "I remember being told about the ring, but I can't remember exactly the details of what made it particularly special."

Paloma frowned. How did Gael and Lizzie not know this? The peacock ring had to have been stolen two weeks ago. She wanted to write down everything Tavo's father said on a note card.

"Paloma, my dear, what made you ask about a ring?" Mr. Farill asked, snapping Paloma out of her thoughts. A wave of panic hit her hard. She was talking too much. Lulu

Pennywhistle always warned, "Too much schmooze loses the clues."

Paloma pulled on her side braid and shrugged. "You said jewelry, so I just thought about rings. I love rings."

Mr. Farill nodded and looked at his watch. "It's a great injustice. Now, if you two don't mind, I must go upstairs. I promised Mrs. Farill that I'd meet her at the Rodin exhibit. See you both in the lobby in an hour. Enjoy."

As soon as his dad was out of earshot, Tavo lightly bumped shoulders with Paloma. "Whoa, my dad really likes you. He never talks to me about art like that. You've totally impressed him."

"I did?" Paloma said, surprised. "Your dad knows a lot." Paloma dug into her bag for a note card and pen. She didn't want to forget a single detail. "I'm going to jot down some notes."

"Paloma Marquez, you're such an art nerd!" Tavo laughed.

Paloma smiled at him and chuckled but kept writing. "If I am, it's because you're the one who nerded out on me that first night at the reception talking about Frida. It's contagious."

Tavo laughed some more and snagged her note card once she finished writing.

"Hey!" Paloma protested, but let him read it. It was just notes about the painting. He wouldn't suspect she was up to anything else—like hunting for a peacock ring.

Tavo smiled as his eyes darted across the note card. "You forgot to note down the year of the painting." He handed it back to her.

"That's right," Paloma said. She snatched the card back and wrote down "1941." "Timing is important," she muttered. Then another thought hit her. What about the timing of the peacock ring?

She pulled out a few more of her note cards. Did the ring go missing in 1954, when Frida died, or did Diego hide it somewhere else before he died in 1957? Did the peacock ring disappear after they opened the secret room in 2004? Or did it get taken two weeks ago during the robbery?

Two weeks ago. Paloma let the words soak in like a stroke of paint. Tavo drifted off to admire another painting, and that was Paloma's chance to search through her cards. She was sure she had notes about other occurrences two weeks ago. She made a list as she rummaged through her note cards.

"More notes, Paloma?" Tavo teased from two paintings away.

She forced a cheesy smile and shrugged. "I love art! Can't get enough." Tavo shook his head, and Paloma went back to her cards. She made a list of everything that happened two weeks ago:

There was a robbery at Casa Azul and a man went to jail.

The Fortune-Teller arrived in Coyoacán.

Gael and Lizzie bought medallions for protection.

Gael and Lizzie's father left for New York City.

Paloma wasn't sure how it was all connected, but Lulu Pennywhistle didn't believe in coincidences and neither did Paloma. There was only one way to know for certain.

"Everything okay?" Tavo asked, wandering back over to her.

Paloma felt her face go hot as she shoved her list into her bag. "I need to find your dad for a minute," she said.

Before Tavo could say anything more, Paloma bolted up the passageway to the sixth floor. She found Tavo's father just as he paused outside the exhibit of Rodin sculptures.

"Mr. Farill," she said, out of breath from the run. He turned around, surprised to see her.

"Paloma, is everything okay?" he asked.

"I'm sorry to bother you, but you said the guy who stole Frida's things was in jail, right? Who was he? Do you know his name by any chance?"

Mr. Farill nodded. "Yes, his name is on the tip of my tongue. I believe it was Antonio . . . Antonio Castillo."

Paloma staggered back, in shock. "Castillo? Are you sure?"

"Yes, I'm certain," Mr. Farill said, and then put a hand on her shoulder. "Everything okay? Why do you ask?"

Paloma stiffened. She felt like she might pass out right there.

"No reason. I just thought it'd be an interesting story to share with my mom."

He gave her one last gentle smile and walked off toward the exhibit with all the Rodin sculptures. Paloma felt as frozen in place as the sculptures looked.

Soon, Tavo approached. His mouth opened and closed as he talked excitedly about something, but Paloma couldn't process anything he said. She managed a faint smile while her stomach knotted up. Could it be true?

Gael and Lizzie's dad wasn't in New York City. He was in jail.

Chapter 19

Self-Portrait of a Clueless Paloma

During the car ride home, Paloma's head spun through every conversation she'd had with Gael and Lizzie about their father. Several times she had felt like they were hiding something from her or not telling her the truth. It was a gut feeling she ignored because they were her friends. Now Paloma felt foolish. The truth had been there the whole time.

Paloma shuddered as she connected the pieces. The way Paloma saw it was once Mr. Castillo was caught for stealing from Casa Azul, he was thrown in jail. Losing their dad to jail, Gael and Lizzie suddenly felt afraid. That's why they bought the Aztec eagle warrior medallions and a crucifix from the Fortune-Teller. That's why Gael said he only spoke to his dad every other week.

Paloma felt like her head would explode.

Yet, there were still two burning questions she couldn't answer: If their dad stole the peacock ring, then why were they looking for it? And why did they involve her in any of it?

Once the car parked in front of her house, Tavo walked her inside the gate. Paloma looked back over her shoulder toward the planter. She hoped Gael had left her a note.

"Is everything okay?" Tavo asked. "You were super quiet on the ride home."

"I think looking at all that art has drained my brain," Paloma said, adding a weak laugh. She felt bad that she hadn't been better company to Tavo. He'd been nothing but honest and sweet, and instead of enjoying time with him, she'd been focused on Gael and Lizzie. "I'm just super exhausted."

"Get some rest. Maybe we can meet later this week for churros after your classes or something?"

"Sure," Paloma said, mustering a weak smile. She hesitated before going into the house, and waited for the Farills' car to disappear down the street. Once it was gone, she rushed over to the planter and shoved the stems and leaves aside to check for a note from Gael, but there was none. As she stomped back toward the house, Professor Breton suddenly opened the front door.

"Hey, Paloma, welcome back. How was the museum?"

"It was good," Paloma answered, looking around the house. She could hear her mom in another room on the phone, sounding very stressed out.

"Just good? Not fantastic?" Professor Breton teased. "Did you take a lot of pictures for—"

"What's up with Mom?" Paloma interrupted. "She sounds upset." Paloma bit down on her lip. Were Gramps and Nana okay?

"Well, it's not good news, I can tell you that much," Professor Breton said, shaking his head. "And it's my fault."

"What do you mean?" Paloma's mind raced. Was her mom losing her fellowship?

"She's on the phone with some university folks. It's about your friends Gael and Lizzie, but let's wait for her."

Paloma's heart stopped at the mention of Gael's and Lizzie's names. Soon her mom rushed into the living room. "This is just crazy." She took Paloma's hands and sat her down across from her on the living room couch.

"Tell me what's wrong," Paloma said.

"Okay, so you know how I was planning to call Gael and Lizzie's parents about you guys sneaking out, right?"

"Oh, Mom! Why do you have to—?"

"Before you whine and moan, you need to hear this. I called some friends of mine who work at the university to inquire about how to reach Mr. Castillo by phone, and they've never heard of him."

Paloma looked back and forth from Professor Breton to her mom. She hoped her face didn't give away that she knew where they were heading.

"They have no record of his being at the university, or a visiting artist, or anything."

"Then I remembered that your mom had told me that Gael and Lizzie hung out by the churro stand," Professor Breton jumped in. "So we went and talked to Gael's aunt. She says that their father isn't an artist in New York. He's in jail accused of stealing from Casa Azul. They're living with her right now. That's all she would tell us. Frankly, I was surprised. The newspapers had reported a case of vandalism at Casa Azul a few weeks ago but not a robbery. That's why the museum has installed security cameras. Anyway, it's a big mess."

Paloma pulled on her side braid and wrapped it around her index finger over and over. When Mr. Farill told her the name of the thief, she didn't want to believe it. Paloma had kept a little spark of hope that it would be another Antonio Castillo, but it was true.

"The aunt said that he's innocent, but of course she'd say that," her mom added, and let out a long sigh. "There's more, too."

"More? What else?" Paloma asked.

"That got us thinking about Gael and Lizzie. Since they lied to us about their father . . . maybe they were lying about other stuff, too."

"Are you serious?" Paloma covered her face with her hands.

"So I went online to check their names in the language program registrar," Professor Breton said. "It turns out they're not even listed in the program! I called one of my colleagues who works with the program. He confirmed that they're not in the program. They're not supposed to be tutoring you. I feel horrible."

"They're little imposters!" Paloma's mom said, throwing her hands up in the air in frustration.

"But . . ." she started. Paloma had no words. She looked up at Professor Breton for an explanation.

"I'm so sorry, Paloma. The night of the reception, Gael mentioned the language program. I'm certain he said he was part of it and was there to meet you. His English was excellent. I saw no reason to question it."

Paloma's brain was buzzing. She had to talk to Gael.

"I'm the one to blame," Paloma's mom said. She brushed the bangs away from Paloma's eyes. "Here I was encouraging you to hang out with those two, and this whole time, they've just been a couple of little tricksters."

"No, they're not," Paloma mumbled, feeling the weight of the entire day on her shoulders. Her brain hurt. Her heart hurt, too. Sure, the Castillos had lied to her. But they'd been so nice to her, too. She couldn't dismiss them without hearing their side of the story first. "They're my friends. I have to talk to Gael. Can I please have my phone back?"

"Absolutely not, Paloma Jane! Did you not hear what I said?" Her mom stood up and walked a few steps away with her arms crossed over her chest. "They're hustlers. They came to our house with pastries. They sell this story about their father being an artist away in New York. They serenade us, but then they have you sneak out of the house for churros, and now this!"

"They didn't make me do anything," Paloma said with a quick eye roll. "They must have a good reason. I'm sure of it."

Paloma stomped to her bedroom. She paced the room, pulling on her eagle warrior medallion. She still believed it protected her, but she wasn't sure she believed in Gael anymore.

She opened her memory box and touched the purple flower she had worn in her hair the first night they met. Gael said that wearing a purple flower in her hair was something Frida would do. He had also told her that he had chosen her to help solve the mystery with him because he agreed with what she said about "not being fake," but that wasn't true. He's been a mega-super faker this whole time—and Paloma was going to find out why.

Chapter 20

A Big Fat *Mentira*

For two days, Paloma left notes for Gael inside the planter, asking him to come see her at school. Every day she checked, her notes were gone, but there was never a note in return. During the break between classes on Tuesday, she heard Gael's and Lizzie's laughter before she even saw them.

Paloma bolted out the school entrance and then paused on the stairs to watch them. Lizzie was standing, and Gael was sitting. Both of them were finishing Popsicles. Gael let out a snort-laugh, and Lizzie convulsed into loud joyful cackles. They seemed happy, like they had no cares in the world. They didn't seem like kids whose father was in jail.

"Paloma!" Gael shouted once he spotted her. He rushed

up to her, and Lizzie followed. Gael kissed her cheek and then pushed an orange Popsicle in her face.

"You have to try this. You probably don't have these in Kansas."

Paloma stepped back. "What is it?"

"A mango *paleta*. With *chile*," Gael said. "It's sweet and spicy just like us."

Paloma winced and took a bite. It was good until she got to the chili pepper. She made a sour face that sent Gael into a laughing fit.

Lizzie shook her head at Gael and handed Paloma a bottle of water.

"Obviously, I'm the sweet part," she said, and then took a few steps back from Paloma, who looked like she might cry. "*¡No llores!* Don't cry! It wasn't that spicy, was it, Paloma?"

"It's not the chili. Did you guys get the notes that I've left in the planter for you for the last two days? I needed to talk about something important."

"What notes?" Gael said. He and Lizzie exchanged blank looks and shook their heads. "We stopped by both days and didn't see a note from you."

"How did you know to meet me here, then?"

"Because you always have a break at this time and we missed seeing you," Gael answered. "We thought you'd like a *paleta*."

Paloma didn't know whether to smile because they had missed her and brought her a *paleta* or to scream at them because they were one big phony charade.

"Maybe you guys can tell me how to say 'lie' in *español*?" Paloma hissed.

"We say '*mentira*.' Why, Paloma? What's happened?" Gael asked with a face so innocent and sweet, Paloma felt bad for bringing it up. She had Gael spell it for her on a note card.

"*Mentira,*" she said, holding the card in front of them. "Both of you have been lying to me about the peacock ring and your father." Paloma stopped as Gael let out a deep breath. He looked like a deflating blowfish. Lizzie looked down at her black ballet flats. "You told me your dad was in New York, but he's really in jail. My mom spoke to your aunt at the churro stand. I know it was your dad who stole the ring."

"No, Paloma," Gael said, shaking his head. "That is not the truth. You're right. We haven't been one hundred percent honest, but we will tell you everything right now. The honest-to-God truth."

Paloma wasn't sure she could believe anything they said now. She looked around and noticed students heading back into the school with their snacks and juices.

"We don't want you to get into trouble," Gael said. "We can wait for you here after class."

Paloma looked back toward the school. If she didn't go now, she'd miss some of her Spanish class, but Gael shifted around like a squirmy fish she'd just caught. If she left now, he might just swim off. Leaving her with no answers.

She sat down on the bench. "Tell me the truth," she said.

"Our father is Antonio Castillo," Gael said. "He isn't an artist. He's an art teacher, but he lost his teaching job because of government cuts. Anyway, he found work at the museum helping to catalog all the jewelry and dresses discovered in Frida's secret room. Many people were hired to go through it. They worked to have it ready for exhibit and to preserve it."

Paloma nodded.

"Our dad was doing his work, and he noticed that a ring that had been recorded was suddenly missing. He told his boss. Two days later, his boss was transferred to another museum in Guadalajara. My dad spoke to him before he left and he urged our dad to just forget it, but our dad couldn't. He continued to ask people about it. He even called the police to report it missing." Gael's head dropped, and his shoulders slumped. "That was his big mistake."

"What happened?" Paloma asked.

"Our dad received a phone call from someone he thought was the museum director," Lizzie said, continuing the story. "He invited our dad to meet him at a market in Mexico City for lunch to discuss a full-time job with the museum. Our dad believed he had done the right thing, and he thought that he was being recognized for it with a job offer but he was wrong. At the market, a man our dad didn't know offered him thousands of dollars to be quiet about the missing ring."

"The man was trying to bribe him," Gael said in disgust. "Our dad refused. He told the man that he would talk to the press. He tried to leave, but the man threatened him. My dad knocked the man down. He was leaving when the police arrived. The man accused our dad of stealing Frida's jewelry. They searched our dad's bag and found a jade necklace. My dad didn't know how it got in there. He never stole anything. Someone put the necklace in his bag. This man told police that our dad had shown up there to sell the necklace to him illegally. He lied. Our dad was an art teacher. He would never do that to Frida or to the museum."

"He's not a thief," Lizzie added. She flashed a photo on her phone in front of Paloma. Paloma took it from her. It was a picture of Gael, Lizzie, and their dad in front of the coyote fountain in the Jardín Centenario. In their dad's soft, smiling eyes, Paloma could see an older Gael. Paloma handed the photo back to Lizzie.

"You have his eyes," Paloma said softly.

"And his *corazón*," Gael added, touching his heart.

"So if your dad didn't steal the peacock ring, you . . ." Paloma trailed off, trying to put the pieces together. "You think you can find it and free your dad from jail?"

Lizzie and Gael nodded.

"He's only allowed visitors every other week. He's told us everything that happened, but he doesn't know that we're looking for the ring. He can't know. He worries about us because the man who trapped him is very powerful and can hire people to hurt us."

"Hurt you? Is that why you bought the Aztec eagle medallion and the crucifix from the Fortune-Teller?" Paloma asked.

Gael and Lizzie exchanged a puzzled look.

"She told me that you both seemed desperate and that you wanted them for protection."

"He's dangerous. He will come after us if he thinks we're trying to help our dad. Our dad will never be free unless we can find the ring and expose the real thief."

"So then why was the Trench Coat Man lurking around if he already has the ring? Why hasn't he already left town with it?" Paloma asked. "That's who you're talking about, right? The Trench Coat Man? He framed your father?"

Gael and Lizzie both shook their heads.

"No, Paloma," Gael said, stepping closer to her. He looked around to ensure no one was close by to overhear him. "We still don't know who the Trench Coat Man is or why he was at Casa Azul. The real thief is Tavo's father, Mr. Farill."

Chapter 21

What Is the Truth?

Paloma stood there stunned for a few seconds before throwing her hands up over her head. "Are you guys out of your minds? That can't be right. He loves Frida. You should hear how he talks about her. He—"

"He framed our father," Gael said. Paloma shook her head. It was too hard to believe. "He's hidden the ring for now until his smuggler can do his part. Our dad told us."

"Smuggler?" Paloma asked.

"The Trench Coat Man," Lizzie said. "We think Mr. Farill is working with him to collect the ring and get it out of Mexico. He was there at Casa Azul that night and we think he's watching us in the black car."

"But," Paloma started. "If he's the smuggler . . . why

hang around, lurking at Casa Azul? He should take the ring and go, you know?"

"We thought about that, too," Lizzie said. "Maybe he's waiting for the right time to take the ring."

"Mr. Farill is *importante* in this town. He donates to churches, museums, and universities," Gael added. "Everyone thinks he's a saint. Even your mom loves him, right? He paid for her fellowship. This is the mask he wears. He can't be caught with the ring. He hires thugs like the Trench Coat Man to do his dirty work."

Paloma felt suddenly woozy. "What did you say about a mask?" she asked.

"He's a faker who wears a mask," Gael repeated.

Gael's words rushed over Paloma like a brushstroke of bright red. Paloma's mind shot back to the dinner at the Farills', when Tavo's mom mentioned that it was Mr. Farill's idea to make Frida's party a masquerade. She complained that it was a last-minute change made just two weeks ago. Two weeks ago! Isn't that what she said?

"What's going on in your head?" Gael asked. "I see it working, Paloma. You know we're right."

"Frida's party is going to be a *baile de máscaras*. It was Mr. Farill's idea," Paloma said. "What's his motive for making it a masquerade party at the last minute?" Paloma stood up now. She paced the sidewalk. Lulu always said that a little exercise gets the brain humming.

"He's a jerk. That's his motive," Lizzie said. Paloma ignored her comment.

"I know!" Gael said. "Maybe he's planning to steal again at the night of Frida's party—"

"If Casa Azul is full of guests wearing masks, the cameras can't identify him or the Trench Coat Man," Paloma said.

Gael suddenly hugged her. "You believe us?"

Paloma frowned and stepped back from his embrace. It felt wrong to suspect Mr. Farill. He had been so kind to her. He paid for her mom's trip to Mexico. He was Tavo's father. Still, Paloma couldn't ignore the evidence: Mr. Castillo told Gael and Lizzie it was Mr. Farill. As if that wasn't enough, Mr. Farill admitted that it was his idea to change the party to a masquerade. Plus, there was another clue that nagged Paloma. Her mind shot back to the day at the museum when Tavo told her that her father was against the security cameras being installed at Casa Azul. Mr. Farill argued that it was because it would destroy the dignity of Frida's home, but maybe that wasn't the whole truth.

"After your dad was caught with the jade necklace . . ." Paloma said, piecing together a timeline. "The management at Casa Azul decided to install cameras. Mr. Farill was against it. I know this because he told me himself when we were on our trip. When he saw that they'd installed them, he had his wife change Frida's party to a masquerade. A last-minute change."

"That's right!" Lizzie said. "They started installing cameras outside right after our dad was sent to jail. They're installing them inside, too. I saw them at mariachi practice."

"That's why he wants everyone to wear masks," Paloma said. "He could be planning something the night of the party."

"Who needs Lulu Pennywhistle when we've got you?" Gael gushed.

Paloma couldn't smile. She was still annoyed with their lies. Instead, she focused back on her two burning questions. First, if their father stole the peacock ring, why were they looking for it?

She had her answer now. According to Gael and Lizzie, he didn't steal it. He was framed. Now they were trying to find it and set their dad free.

The second question still remained: Why did Gael and Lizzie involve her in this? Paloma's stomach tightened into a knot.

"Tell me this, were you ever my true friends?"

Gael stepped back like she'd just taken a swing at him. "What do you mean?"

"Of course we're your friends," Lizzie said in an offended tone.

"Are you? That first night we saw each other. The night of the reception in Frida's studio, I know that you guys were listening to Tavo and me. You probably overheard me say that I love mysteries. You probably overheard Tavo say how we're going to spend a lot of time together. Didn't you? You wrote me that stupid note with the crazy-sketched eye because . . . because Mr. Farill is Tavo's father? I'm right, aren't I?" Paloma shook her head and sat back down on the bench.

"Yes," Lizzie said softly. Gael shot her an angry look. "It's why I didn't want you involved. I didn't feel right using you to get information about the Farills."

"That's why you were so rough with me? Told me I was a simple Kansas girl?"

Lizzie nodded. "But you proved me wrong," she said with so much sincerity in her voice that Paloma wanted to hug her. She wished she could forget all about this and be their friend again.

"Since Tavo was taking an interest in you, I thought through you we could learn where they lived. Even though our dad thinks Mr. Farill has the ring hidden at Casa Azul, Lizzie and I thought it might be at his home, but now we're not so sure," Gael explained.

Paloma let her head drop back in frustration. "That *was* you in the taxi behind me that night my mom and I went to dinner at their house. I knew it!"

Gael nodded.

"What were you doing?"

"We wanted to know where they lived and how tricky it would be to get past security," Gael admitted.

A thousand alarms went off in Paloma's head, but still she pressed on. "Why?" she asked, bracing herself for his answer.

Gael looked down at his feet. Paloma turned to Lizzie. Lizzie picked at her long dark braid and avoided Paloma's gaze.

"No more lies," Paloma warned them. "I deserve to know the truth."

Gael let out a deep breath. "The truth is we needed to know where Tavo lived so we could get inside his house to find the ring, but even though we searched, we didn't find anything."

Paloma steadied herself on the bench with her hands. They were the ones responsible for breaking into Tavo's home. In one quick motion, she pulled the Aztec eagle soldier medallion off over her head. She felt strange without it, but thrust it at Gael.

"Take it," she said, forcing it into the palm of his hand.

"Please, Paloma," Gael said. "We didn't want to lie to you, but we have to help our dad. He's innocent and we love him. Will you still help us, now that you know the truth?" Gael said, extending the medallion back to her.

"You said you wanted my help because of what I said about Frida's painting: She was telling us not to be fake in our lives."

"I believe that with my whole *corazón*, but it's our dad we're talking about," Gael said, placing a hand over his heart. "I'm sorry for the lies."

"We both are," Lizzie added.

Paloma stood up to go and then stopped. "I'm sorry about your dad," she said. Paloma turned back toward the school's doors. With every step she took, a sharp pain shot across her chest. She knew what it was like to want your father back. Paloma would give anything for another day with hers, for even one true memory of him.

Chapter 22

The Gold Cuff Link

Paloma felt zapped of energy. Her chest thumped hard like a chisel was hacking away at her heart, leaving it in pieces. She walked toward Spanish class, but halfway there she turned around, unwilling to practice vocabulary for an hour. She already knew the most important words and expressions.

Mentira—a lie
Lo siento—I'm sorry
Amigos—friends
Adiós—good-bye

She headed out of the school, toward the street, and jumped on the first bus that came her way. A few minutes later, it dropped her off a couple of blocks from Casa Azul. As she walked toward Frida's home, Gael's words replayed in her head: "We didn't want to lie to you, but we have to help our dad. He's innocent and we love him. Will you still help us, now that you know the truth?"

Paloma rubbed her forehead. It felt rotten to be lied to. It felt rotten to lose friends. She entered the museum and walked over to one of the staff at the door. She asked where she could find Frida's *My Dress Hangs There* painting. The woman directed her to the first floor.

Face-to-face with her father's favorite Frida Kahlo painting, Paloma soaked in the image of Frida's colorful dress dangling from a clothesline in the middle of New York City. All around the dainty dress were New York skyscrapers, Lady Liberty, and images of people marching. Paloma squeezed her eyes shut and imagined herself as the dress, dangling and swaying from a clothesline above the city of Coyoacán. In her mind, Gael and Lizzie held one end of the clothesline. On the other side, Tavo and his parents held the other end.

"Paloma?" Tavo called out to her. She opened her eyes to see him walking toward her. "You just can't get enough of Frida now, huh? You're like a true-blue Fridanista!"

Paloma prayed he couldn't hear her heart pounding in her chest. She felt guilty knowing now who broke into his home. She was the one who led them there. It was all done behind her back, but still the guilt was like a hot, scratchy blanket she wanted to shrug off but couldn't. She smiled and tried to breathe like a normal person.

"Fridanista. I like that. I'm going to write that one down," she said, and pulled out a note card and pen.

"You and those note cards," Tavo snickered. "What are you doing here anyway?"

"This was my dad's favorite Frida Kahlo painting. So I came to pay tribute."

Tavo dug his hands into his pockets. "It's a good one. She painted this while she was in New York City with Diego. She was super homesick for Mexico. It's crammed with symbolism."

"Maybe my dad was homesick for Mexico, too," Paloma said, taking a deep breath.

"I know your dad died when you were young. Your mom mentioned it at dinner. Is it hard to be without him?"

"It just feels like something is missing sometimes." Paloma paused, unsure if "missing" was the right word for how she felt. "And you? What are you doing here?" she asked. "Can't get enough of Frida, either?"

"I came with my mom. She's meeting with the party committee. It's only a week away. And while she's doing that, I came inside because my dad lost something here. My mom and I thought maybe it was taken during the break-in, but he insists that it's here at Casa Azul. He's here all the time meeting with the staff about different art projects and exhibits. You know adding the gift shop was my dad's idea. He thought the museum could make money selling Frida magnets and coffee cups."

"The gift shop was your dad's idea?" Paloma narrowed her eyes. "That's so weird." Tavo gave her a puzzled look. "Remember when I told you I bumped into your dad here with my tutor . . ."

Tavo nodded.

"He was over by the cafeteria. Anyway, he told me he got lost looking for the gift shop."

"That's ridiculous," Tavo said, rolling his eyes. "My dad and mom know this place inside and out. He was obviously having a senior moment."

Paloma chuckled, but inside she fumed. What was Mr. Farill really doing near the locked storage room? More proof that Mr. Farill was not as innocent as Paloma had first thought. Her mind wandered to Gael. Was that why he was so curious about that back area when he saw Mr. Farill come from there? And then after their run-in with the Trench Coat Man, did he decide that the ring wasn't at Casa Azul and that led them to sneaking into Mr. Farill's home?

"Have the police figured out who broke into your home?" Paloma asked. "Any new information?"

"Turns out it was two kids dressed up as cleaners."

Paloma felt a jolt of fear for Gael and Lizzie. As mad as she was at them, they didn't deserve to be in jail.

"You can identify them?"

"Nah, they were smart. It's like they knew about our

cameras. They wore surgical masks and caps. They even used our maid's cleaning gloves, too. Sneaky. Still, they didn't take anything. You'll be happy to know the creepy Picasso painting is safe."

"Yay!" Paloma said with as much sarcasm as she could muster. She knew all along Gael and Lizzie weren't thieves, but she was relieved to hear it.

"My room was untouched. My mom said it was as if they were looking for something specific. Anyway, my dad was crazy angry. He'll do what he usually does. He won't stop until someone is fired or arrested. That will be the end of it."

Paloma stepped back, offended. Is that what Mr. Farill had done to Mr. Castillo? Freaked out and got him arrested?

Suddenly, a lady walked up with a cardboard box. "Mr. Farill. This is the lost-and-found box. We've looked through it for the cuff link, but maybe you'd like to double-check?"

Tavo nodded and took the box from her, placing it on a display table. "Thank you," he responded to the woman. He dug through various knickknacks in the box. Paloma leaned in to help.

"What does it look like?" she asked.

"It's gold. Very old," he said. "It's been handed down from my great-great-grandfather to my dad. It's a unique piece that looks like an old-fashioned peso coin."

Paloma stiffened at Tavo's description. She'd seen a cuff link like that before. Twice in fact. When she and Tavo took the selfie in front of the creepy Picasso, she saw it on the high-top table. There was just one. The match had to be the one that she and Gael found in the storage room, near one of the wheelchairs. Paloma's mind raced to remember what she'd done with it. Jeans' pocket! It had to be in her black jeans' pocket. Paloma chewed on her bottom lip.

"I have to go," she said.

"So soon? Do you want a ride home?" Tavo asked. "Our driver is parked outside."

Paloma waved back at him as she exited the gallery. "I'm good. Thanks!"

She darted out of the museum toward the cafeteria. Mr. Farill had told her he was lost looking for the gift shop when he came out from behind the cafeteria. It was a massive lie. He was in the storage room, and he lost his gold cuff link inside.

Why would Mr. Farill and the Trench Coat Man be so interested in a stupid storage room unless there was something valuable hidden there? Paloma's heart raced as she realized what she must do. There was no time to waste. As she crossed the courtyard, a large mariachi group began to practice. Trumpets blared. Guitars thrummed. The violins began to crescendo. Men's voices sang into microphones, filling the courtyard with *"¡Ay, ay, ay!"*

Before she slipped through the transparent tarp that led to the far end of the courtyard and the secret room, she scanned the area for security guards. There were none in sight. This was her chance. She grabbed a big rock and took it behind the tree. The storage room door was locked. She banged at the lock with the stone, but it didn't move. She struck it over and over. Still it wouldn't break. She grabbed a bobby pin from her hair to maneuver it into the lock, but it didn't open. Feeling defeated, she sunk down to the ground and threw the rock at the base of the tree. When it struck the ground, Paloma expected a soft thud, but instead it made a metallic sound.

Paloma got up and walked over to the base of the tree. She grabbed the stone and tapped it on the ground. *Ting, ting, ting.* When she brushed away the dirt and wet mud caused by the rain the night before, Paloma couldn't believe her eyes. There, under the tree, was a metal box. It was buried in the mud. Digging her fingers into the wet ground, Paloma tried to nudge it loose and pull it out, but it wouldn't budge. Instead, she left it stuck in the mud and opened the simple latch. Inside was a small gold key and an invitation for Frida's party. Over Frida's face, someone had scribbled in thick black ink:

Las Mañanitas 8:15

Chapter 23

Supersleuth Paloma

Paloma couldn't believe her eyes. She knew enough Spanish to know that *"mañana"* meant "morning." Did Mr. Farill leave it for the Trench Coat Man to get the key the day of Frida's party at 8:15 in the morning? Paloma rubbed her forehead. That didn't seem right. Why would he take that risk in daylight? She'd have to figure it out later. Right now, the gold key was in the palm of her hand. Paloma got up and stepped toward the door. She slid the key into the lock and turned it until it clicked. From over the top of the cafeteria, she could hear the mariachi continue to belt out songs. With a quick glance back toward the tree to make sure she was still alone, she tapped the door open and stepped in, stashing the key and lock in her front jean pocket.

The room was dark, but she remembered that there was a dangling lightbulb. She treaded farther into the room and yanked the string to the light. The yellow glow was enough for her to once again see the ladders, metal buckets, the desk she and Gael hid under, and a wheelchair covered with dusty old blankets.

Her eyes darted around the room, taking in every dark, dusty corner. Something as small as a ring could be anywhere. Where would Mr. Farill hide it? Her mind raced back to that scary night in the room with Gael. Before the whole Trench Coat Man attack, she had found the gold cuff link on the ground near the wheelchair. She pushed the wheelchair back and squatted down to run her hands along the tiled floor. A few small black insects scurried out of her path, stopping her heart for a second. After a brief moment to catch her breath, she once again glided her hand along the floor. That's when she felt a loose tile. She gently lifted it up. Beneath the tile was a deep hole. Paloma hesitated. What if there were snakes down there? What if a rat and its baby rats were in that hole waiting for a tasty bite of a human hand?

Paloma glanced around the room for some sort of stick to reach into the hole. There was nothing.

"Okay," Paloma said to herself. "I need to just Lulu up and do this."

She took a deep breath and dipped her hand into the hole. She was elbow-deep when she touched a velvety soft pouch. The pouch held something small, but it had heft.

Paloma grasped the pouch with both hands, pulled it out, and untied it quickly.

From the pouch, she pulled out a small wooden box. A lump formed in Paloma's throat. Her fingers trembled as she opened it. Inside, a silver peacock ring with sparkling emerald and blue sapphire encrusted feathers glimmered. Paloma gasped. She'd found it! She couldn't believe she was holding the ring that Frida Kahlo designed only a few days before she died.

"Wow, Frida," Paloma said softly. "You did it."

After her mom's red opal wedding ring, it was the most gorgeous piece of jewelry Paloma had ever set eyes on. She wiped a tear from her cheek. Suddenly, a thought struck her: If she was caught with the ring right now, then she could never expose Mr. Farill for the thief he was. Worse, Mr. Castillo would remain in jail. She'd have to get it to a safe hiding place quickly. Paloma put the ring back into its box and slipped it in her pocket. Then she replaced the tile and the wheelchair. Quickly, she locked the storage door behind her and returned the gold key to its metal case.

She couldn't let Mr. Farill or the Trench Coat Man take this ring from the museum. It belonged at Frida's home so everyone could see what she created. It wasn't for sale!

Paloma hurried out from behind the cafeteria. She couldn't stop shaking. She had found Frida's peacock ring. It was in her pocket! Now she needed a plan. She scurried toward the courtyard exit when she spotted a camera glowering at her from a tree. It was all starting to make sense. Casa Azul would be full of masked people for the party. The invitation was a clue that whatever Mr. Farill was planning was happening the day of the party, but when exactly? At 8:15 in the morning?

Paloma had almost reached the exit when the mariachi band began another song. The song's lyrics stopped her cold.

Estas son las mañanitas

que cantaba el rey David

She stood to listen a little bit more. What was that song? She tapped a young woman working at the exit turnstile and asked her the name of it.

"'*Las mañanitas,*'" she answered. "They're rehearsing for Frida's birthday party."

"'*Las mañanitas,*'" Paloma repeated. "They're going to sing it at Frida's party?"

"*¡Claro!* It's the birthday song," she said.

"*¡Muchas gracias!*"

Paloma sprinted home. She was mentally moving the different pieces together to see how they fit. Paloma was convinced that something was definitely going down at Frida's birthday celebration at Casa Azul. Something at 8:15 during the singing of *"Las mañanitas."* This had to be what the note meant.

At home, Paloma rummaged through her laundry, looking for her black jeans. She pulled them out of the hamper and dug through the back pockets. The cuff link was cold against her fingertips. She pulled it out. It was exactly as Tavo had described. More importantly, it was a clear match with the cuff link she'd seen at Tavo's house when they took their selfie. Paloma's mind raced with theories. Each one linked Mr. Farill to the storage room where the peacock ring was hidden. Was he hiding it there while waiting for his smuggler, the Trench Coat Man, to take it? Was that why the Trench Coat Man was at the museum that night? Had he come to collect the ring, but was forced to give up when Paloma and Gael got in his way?

Paloma had more questions than answers, but at least she found the peacock ring. Without her phone, Paloma had no choice but to run to the churro stand and hope Gael and Lizzie were there. She had so much to tell them.

As soon as she arrived at the Jardín Centenario, Paloma spotted Gael and Lizzie getting into a cab. She ran to the corner to catch them. A car turned in front of her, cutting her off. She yelled for Gael, but he didn't hear her.

Where are they going? A couple of taxis passed her by, and Paloma patted the bag slung across her chest. She had spending money from her grandparents. She threw her hands up to hail a taxi. As soon as one stopped for her, Paloma jumped into the backseat. The driver turned around to ask her for directions.

"*¿A dónde, mi reina?*"

Paloma worked her brain to find the vocabulary she

wanted and form the words in her mouth. She had to tell him where to go, but she didn't know where Gael and Lizzie were heading. She racked her head for the words "follow" and "taxi." In an instant it came to her.

"*¡Siga ese taxi! Por favor,*" Paloma said. The driver nodded.

After a fifteen-minute drive through Coyoacán toward Mexico City, it was obvious to Paloma that Gael and Lizzie's taxi was following another cab. It turned when the taxi in front of them turned. Their taxi slowed when the other taxi slowed. Who were they following?

Paloma kept her eyes on both taxis ahead of her as they snaked through streets. A small boy dressed in ripped, dirty clothes tapped on the taxi driver's window to sell them candy. Another boy was selling chips. This was a part of Mexico City Paloma hadn't seen.

As Gael and Lizzie's taxi suddenly pulled over to a curb, Paloma's taxi lurched to a stop behind it.

"*¡Aquí! Gracias, señor,*" Paloma said to the driver. She handed him a few bills, opened her car door, and half stepped out, when she noticed that Gael and Lizzie were still in the backseat of their car. Gael leaned over Lizzie and pointed out the window. Paloma followed his finger toward a slender man in a dark gray suit, holding a briefcase and striding toward a four-story outdoor market bustling with shoppers.

Paloma covered her mouth with her hand. It was Mr.

Farill! Gael and Lizzie stepped out of the taxi and followed him into the market.

"*¿Todo está bien?*" The taxi driver gave her a puzzled look.

Paloma looked down at her sandals, gray capris, and blue striped shirt. She was dressed for a day at the park with friends—not for spying! She slid out of the taxi anyway and rushed to where she saw Gael and Lizzie enter the market. Paloma had just taken a few steps inside when a woman shoved skeleton puppets at her. The skeletons wore flowers on their heads and bright dresses. The vendor made them dance.

"*Gracias, muy bien,*" Paloma said, not knowing what else to say about the freaky puppet skeletons. She managed to slink away from the vendor and continued through the narrow passageway. She spotted Lizzie's head and followed, meandering deeper into the market and passing tables piled high with T-shirts and jeans, and counters full of gold and silver jewelry. A man shouted at her from his table.

"*¡Ofertas! ¡Ofertas!* Everything good price, *niña.*"

Paloma pressed forward through the throng of shoppers carrying full bags of avocados, onions, and bread, and vendors flashing DVDs, shoes, and large sombreros at her. Through all of this, she locked in on Gael and Lizzie, who had suddenly stopped. They looked to their left and right. Paloma knew right away that they had lost Mr. Farill. Where was he? She scanned the area.

That's when she spotted him to her left. She could barely make him out through the crowd of people standing in front of stalls displaying Mexican-style souvenirs. Paloma moved closer. She pretended to admire a few Mexican dolls and watched Mr. Farill greet a stocky man dressed in a sporty tracksuit. Both men laughed. The man patted Mr. Farill on the shoulder and opened the door for him. Paloma craned her neck and caught a quick glimpse of a dimly lit room with a table before the door closed. Paloma glanced backed toward where she'd seen Gael and Lizzie standing, but they were no longer there.

They were right beside her.

Chapter 24

Fridanistas Unite!

"What are you guys doing here?" Paloma asked.

"We should ask you the same thing, Kansas," Lizzie said, full of attitude that took Paloma by surprise.

"I was searching for you guys. I know for sure that something is going down at Frida's birthday party."

"No, don't you see the deal is going down right now," Gael said with an exasperated tone. "Mr. Farill is in that room right now."

Lizzie nodded. "This is our chance to catch him and bust up their exchange of goods."

Paloma shook her head in disbelief. "Exchange of goods? Where did you even learn that expression? Forget it! I don't want to know. Why do you guys think something is going down now? That stocky dude definitely wasn't the Trench Coat Man."

Gael put his arm around Paloma's shoulders, pulled her away from the closed door, and huddled close to her. "We didn't tell you before, but while we were at the Farills' house looking for the ring, we found an email on the printer. It was a note from a dude named Sergei—"

"A Russian name," Lizzie added. "Probably the Trench Coat Man."

"He instructed Mr. Farill to take a taxi from the Jardín Centenario and meet him here at this market on the first level," Gael said. "Turns out, this is the same place he met our father when he framed him and had him arrested."

Paloma shook her head in annoyance. Why hadn't they shared this email information with her when they spoke outside school?

"We didn't tell you because we figured you would try to stop us or, worse, tell your friend Tavo."

Paloma stepped back, shocked by Gael's words. "I would never do that," she said. "I would never betray you guys like that. I want to help your dad, too."

"*Gracias*, Paloma," Gael said softly. "We'll do whatever it takes."

Paloma nodded to show them that she understood. She glimpsed back toward the closed door.

"What's your plan?" Paloma asked.

182

"We're going to bust through the door and get the peacock ring," Gael said. "Once inside, I'll confront Mr. Farill. I'll stand just like this and tell him, 'Hello, my name is Gael Lorca Castillo. You framed my father. Now you will confess like the scum you are.'" Gael lurched forward toward the door Mr. Farill entered. Paloma tugged him back by his shirt.

"Are you nuts?" Paloma whispered. "You can't just barge in there and say things like that."

"I thought it sounded really good," Gael said with an offended tone, and looked to Lizzie for support.

"You watch too many movies," she said with a smirk.

"Look, say whatever you want, but he doesn't have the peacock ring," Paloma explained. Gael narrowed his eyes at her.

"You still don't believe us? What more proof do you need?"

"No, I totally believe you guys. I just know he doesn't have it . . . because I do. I found it. It's safe in my memory box at home."

Lizzie's and Gael's mouths dropped open in shock.

"I know it's *cray cray*, but I found it!" Paloma gushed. "And it's more beautiful than you can imagine."

"How?" Lizzie asked in wonderment.

"We were right all along. It was in the locked room. But we can't just turn it in. If we do that, we can't prove Mr. Farill is the true criminal. That won't save your father. We have to catch Mr. Farill in the act."

"But they're inside that room right now!" Lizzie said. "We can't just let them get away."

"Now it makes sense to me why you ran off that day when we saw him at Casa Azul," Paloma said to Gael. He nodded. "You left me to pay for the *limonada*. You didn't want him to see you with me. You thought he'd recognize you as the son of the man he framed, right?"

"If he connected us, he'd become suspicious," Gael said.

"You guys can stand out here and talk, but I'm going in!" Lizzie said, and broke off from the group, heading straight toward the closed door.

"She can't do that! Stop her!" Paloma yelled at Gael. He bolted after her, but it was too late. Lizzie turned the doorknob and shoved her body against the door. But the door didn't budge.

"It's locked," she muttered with a frown. "Of course it's locked." Lizzie banged the door with her fist one last time. Gael pulled her away from the door, speaking to her soothingly in Spanish.

They settled on the stairway. Lizzie crossed her arms over her chest. "Every minute that goes by, our dad is stuck in jail, and yet this creep just strolls around the market and throws parties."

Paloma winced. Her heart melted for Gael and Lizzie. It had to be torture knowing that their innocent dad was in jail with real criminals. It was straight-up unfair. She couldn't help but think of her own father. She had a memory box full of photographs of him holding her, taking her for rides on the pony carousel at the mall, and reading picture books to her. All these photographs were wonderful. It proved that he wanted to be with her. But nothing is like having your father by your side. That's what stung Paloma the most. Gael and Lizzie had a dad. He was alive. Yet Mr. Farill was keeping him from his children for his own personal greed. She wasn't so different from Gael and Lizzie. Paloma knew if someone offered her a way to save her dad, she would take it. She'd do anything to have him back at her side forever.

"We're going to catch Mr. Farill," Paloma said with a seriousness that surprised herself. "But we have to be smart. He already has you guys on video. The Farills know it was two kids who entered their home. We can't be reckless."

"What do we do?" Lizzie asked. "He's in there right now. Shouldn't we try to confront him?"

Paloma's eyes darted around the market. "We need to tell the police. If we give them a fake story, maybe they'll open the door for us."

"I got this," Gael said, and raced off. While he was gone, Paloma and Lizzie watched the door to make sure no one left the room.

"Thank you, Kansas," Lizzie said with a smile that Paloma returned. "You know, you always talk about the great Lulu Pennywhistle, but I think someday someone will be writing books about you. I can see it now, supersleuth Paloma Marquez."

Paloma let out a light laugh. "They'll be writing books about all of us someday. Lizzie Castillo, former mariachi extraordinaire becomes Mexico's first female president!"

"And Gael Castillo, the most talented artist of his generation!" Lizzie added.

Gael reappeared with a police officer who looked only a few years older than them. He smiled and nodded a lot.

"I told him how someone stole your phone, Lizzie," Gael said. "And locked themselves in that room."

"You have a true knack for fake stories," Paloma whispered, raising her eyebrows at him.

Gael winked at her and led the young police officer to the door. The officer gave a few polite knocks on the door. After a few seconds, he smiled at the kids and knocked some more. Lizzie pushed her way beside him and pounded on the door with her fist. Still no one answered. The police officer pulled out his baton and gestured for the kids to back up. Once they were clear, he banged the doorknob until it fell off. Then he wedged the door open and peered in.

"Nadie está aquí," he said to the kids with an apologetic look.

Lizzie and Gael pressed forward past the officer and into the room. Paloma followed. Besides a desk and a wire wastebasket, the small room was completely empty. There was no one in sight.

"What mighty high jinks just happened?" Paloma asked. She had seen Mr. Farill enter the room with her own eyes.

They all had. There must be another way out. While Gael sifted through the wastebasket, Paloma and Lizzie glided their hands along the walls until Paloma felt an indentation. Lizzie sidled up to her with her cell phone light. It was a door. Lizzie pressed it forward, and it popped open to a busy street. Paloma stepped back and gasped. "This is seriously straight out of a Lulu Pennywhistle novel."

"How about this? Is this straight out of a Lulu Pennywhistle novel?" Gael asked, waving a note card over his head. "I think I found something of yours." Even though it was dark, Paloma instantly recognized her sketch of the black car. It was the note card she left in the planter with the words "I see you!"

Chapter 25

How to Catch a Thief

A soft breeze swept across Paloma's face. She hadn't meant to leave her bedroom window wide open. She peered over her blanket toward a light tinkling noise that reminded Paloma of the wind chimes on her grandparents' porch in Kansas.

Frida Kahlo sat at the vanity. She was dressed in a long green skirt with white ruffles, a red blouse, and a black shawl. Her bracelets clanked and chimed as she pinned a purple flower in her dark hair.

"I'm dreaming again, aren't I?" Paloma asked, sitting up to face the artist.

"*Sí,*" Frida said, flashing Paloma a vibrant smile. "Dreaming is nice, no? But reality is better."

"Frida, I have to help my friends, but I'm not sure what to do." Paloma stared at Frida. "Do you think I can solve this?"

Frida tilted her head and smiled. "If you believe you can," she said, "you don't need me to tell you."

A tap on the bedroom door startled Paloma awake.

"Frida?" she called out from under the covers. Her eyes darted between the door and the vanity. Frida was gone, the bedroom window latched close. Paloma stirred herself up just as her mom poked her head into her room.

"Get up, sleepy bird. You're going to be late for class."

As the cloudiness of sleep cleared, Paloma wiped her eyes. "I hate mornings," she mumbled back.

"You were talking to Frida Kahlo in your sleep," Paloma's mom said, entering the bedroom and finding a seat at the edge of Paloma's bed.

"I was?" Paloma said with nervous laugh. "Were we chatting about hummingbirds and watermelons?"

Paloma's mom laughed. "I don't know what you were talking about, but you said her name. Now, get up or you'll be late, grouchy bird."

Once her mom left, Paloma scrambled out of her warm bed. She grabbed her memory box and opened it. The peacock ring was still inside, and beneath it, the purple flower she wore in her hair their first night in Coyoacán. It was wilted and flattened now. She dug further until she found the original note Gael had passed her that first night at Casa Azul. Suddenly, she had a plan. She grabbed the note and her Lulu Pennywhistle paperback. Then she threw on clothes and rushed to get to school on time.

Once again, Gael and Lizzie met her outside during break. They needed to create a plan to catch Mr. Farill at Frida's birthday celebration.

"So do you think that Mr. Farill left the key and that note for the Trench Coat Man?"

Paloma nodded. "Probably. I mean, he can't risk being caught with the ring. So he's hired the Trench Coat Man to take it from Casa Azul during the party. '*Las mañanitas*' is his cue to go to the locked room, take the ring, and leave with it. The cameras won't catch him because he'll be in a mask like everyone else. And no one will notice him."

Lizzie nodded excitedly and pulled out a piece of paper from her purse. "Look, we just got this today. It's our performance schedule for the party. We perform twice, but the second time is at eight fifteen p.m. All the mariachi groups will perform '*Las mañanitas*' during the presentation of the birthday cake, just like the note said. It's the perfect time for the Trench Coat Man to make his move because everyone will be singing and getting ready to stuff their faces with cake."

"*¡Exacto!*" Paloma exclaimed. "What Mr. Farill and the Trench Coat Man don't expect is that we will be there to stop them."

"What if Mr. Farill is onto us?" Gael asked. "I mean, he *is* onto us. Finding those note cards yesterday proves it, doesn't it? He knows you've been wanting to talk to us. He knows something is going on, *verdad*?"

Paloma wrinkled her brow. It was true. If Mr. Farill was onto them, they had to take extra precautions. "Just to be safe, you should wear a disguise to the party. There will be mariachis and folkloric dancers there. Gael, can you dress up as a mariachi, too?"

"I'll get him a suit," Lizzie said.

"How will we catch Farill in the act?" Gael asked. "What's the plan?"

Paloma handed him the handwritten note he'd given her the night they met. "Remember how all this mighty high jinks got started? The only way we can catch Mr. Farill in the act is by getting him to bring out the ring. In my Lulu Pennywhistle book, she traps a notorious villain by writing a fake note to convince him that his plan for the night has somehow gone wrong. He is then forced to take action and, in the process, exposes his true wicked self to everyone."

"Lulu is a genius," Gael said. "We can do that, too."

"I like it," Lizzie added.

"Lizzie, we will need you to get us access to a microphone and speaker during the party."

"I'm a mariachi, Kansas. It's no problem!"

"Gael, I'm asking a lot from you. You'll need to get into

the locked room, do a quick switcheroo with the pouch, hide under the desk with our phones in position, and wait for Mr. Farill. What do you think?"

"'Switcheroo'?" Gael asked with a wide smile, pulling out a note card from his pocket. "I can do that." He wrote it down. "We're going to replace the ring with what?"

"I've got something perfect in mind. Leave it to me. I will deliver the note to Mr. Farill long before '*Las mañanitas*' ever plays, confusing him and setting his confession into motion."

"And the Trench Coat Man? What happens to him?"

"Once Mr. Farill is exposed and caught," Paloma said with a shrug, "the Trench Coat Man is Mr. Farill's problem."

Chapter 26

Happy Birthday, Frida!

The night of the party, Paloma tied on a shimmery mask with a peacock feather. With her mask and the white dress her mom picked up for her, she felt transformed. She was no longer Paloma Marquez, regular girl from Kansas and wannabe Lulu Pennywhistle sleuth. She was Paloma Marquez—international tween detective, finder of missing rings, and thief catcher.

As soon as she walked into the living room where her mom and Professor Breton waited, they began to whistle and clap for her. "*¡Ay, Bonita!*" Professor Breton exclaimed.

"Okay, okay." Paloma giggled, holding her hands up for them to stop embarrassing her.

"I had this made for you." Paloma's mom held out a necklace with an opal dangling from a gold chain.

"Your wedding ring!" Paloma gasped.

Her mom latched it around Paloma's neck. "Now it's yours. Something your father touched will always be with you. It's your very own memory."

Paloma touched the coolness of the red opal. The necklace was the most beautiful gift she could even dream of. Paloma gave her mom a long hug.

"Thank you, Mom," she said. "I really love it."

"There's something else," Paloma's mom said. She pulled out Paloma's cell phone from her purse. "Professor Breton says you're his best student, so you've earned it back."

"Thanks!" Paloma exclaimed. She tucked it into her bag as they headed out the door.

At Casa Azul, a mariachi band played outside to welcome guests. Paloma heard the crisp melodic tone of Lizzie's trumpet. She exchanged a quick smile with her friend, who was dressed head to toe in an elegant black-and-silver mariachi suit, including a silver silk mask. Lizzie nodded at Paloma before tipping the trumpet to her lips again.

Paloma followed Professor Breton and her mom into the museum but not before spotting the Fortune-Teller outside hawking her jewelry to guests. Just then, the Farills appeared in front of them, welcoming them to the party with hugs. Paloma barely recognized Mr. Farill behind a golden-jeweled mask that matched Mrs. Farill's. Tavo stood apart from his parents in a purple mask like one of the Teenage Mutant Ninja Turtles wore.

"You look awesome," Tavo said.

Paloma smiled. "Thank you." She felt a pinch of regret that she was going after his father tonight. She had been so anxious to help Gael and Lizzie that she'd forgotten how this whole thing could affect Tavo. Still, what his father was doing to Mr. Castillo was wrong. He had to be stopped.

"Mom, do you mind if we go walk around?" Paloma asked, taking a good glance around the room for Gael. Where was he?

Paloma's mom nudged her playfully. "Go ahead, little bird. Have fun! Just check in with me every once in a while." Paloma nodded and walked off with Tavo.

As Tavo pointed out famous artists and politicians in the courtyard, Paloma kept an eye out for Gael, when suddenly she spied him with the folkloric dancers. He wore the full performance costume, making Paloma giggle. It was the first time she'd seen Gael without his black knit cap. She liked him in the sombrero. He winked at her and gestured to meet him near the punch table.

"I'm going to get punch for us," she told Tavo as he began talking to another boy his age.

She found Gael in front of the punch, pouring two cups for her.

"One for you and one for Tavo," he whispered.

"What happened to the mariachi suit?" Paloma asked, keeping her voice low, too.

Gael rolled his eyes. "Lizzie failed me. She got me a dance suit from one of her friends. Now I have to dance the Jarabe Tapatío with their troupe, so please let's get this whole thing over with as quickly as possible," he said, taking off his sombrero and running his hand through his dark hair.

"Can you get Lizzie and meet me by Frida's pyramid in two minutes?" Paloma asked. Gael nodded and took off.

Tavo was still talking to the boy when Paloma returned to him. She handed him a cup of punch. "I have to find my mom real quick. Be back in a few minutes," she said, and rushed off toward the red-and-yellow pyramid inside Frida's courtyard.

"Over here," Gael whispered. She moved quickly and squatted down beside Lizzie.

"I've got the note ready," Paloma said, and flashed it at them. It was short and sweet. And, hopefully, just intimidating enough to make Mr. Farill feel nervous, run to the storage room, where they planned to catch him on camera holding the pouch, and confess everything on their phones. It worked for Lulu Pennywhistle.

"I've already talked to the DJ. He's a friend and lent me his microphone and speakers," Lizzie announced. "He thinks I'm playing a special song before '*Las mañanitas.*'"

"And I've made the switcheroo," Gael added. "As soon as we're done here, I'll go set up the phones and hide."

"*¡Perfecto!* Good luck to all of us!" Paloma smiled. "Remember, if anything starts going horribly wrong, just do what Lulu does."

"What?" Gael asked.

"Stay awesome and don't let the crook get away." Paloma smiled and handed him her cell phone.

Lizzie rolled her eyes and darted off, but Gael lingered.

"One last thing, Paloma." He pulled the eagle warrior medallion from under his shirt. "I'm giving this back to you for—"

"Protection," she finished for him. She bent her head for him to loop it around her neck. "*Gracias.*"

"No matter what happens tonight, I want you to know that I'm not done knowing you," Gael said. Paloma's heart flipped in her chest. "You're going to fly off to Kansas eventually, but our friendship doesn't end at some imaginary border in the sky. We are birds. Our friendship is our wings. We are going to be part of each other's sky for a long time, okay?"

"Okay," Paloma said softly.

"*Nos vemos*, Paloma," Gael said before rushing off.

Paloma remained crouched, stunned by his words. From across the courtyard, she spotted Mr. Farill with his wife and a couple who Tavo had introduced Paloma to earlier. It was still hard to believe that Mr. Farill could be so wicked when he seemed so kind to her. She stood up, straightened the medallion and red opal pendant around her neck, and peeked at Tavo, who was still chatting it up with a couple of boys.

Paloma knew that whatever happened tonight, Tavo would be hurt. She took a deep breath. Lulu hadn't prepared her for breaking a friend's heart. Paloma glanced again to where she'd seen Mr. Farill, but he wasn't at his wife's side anymore.

She scanned the courtyard for a man in a black tuxedo and gold-jeweled mask. Her heart raced as she realized she couldn't spot him anywhere. Suddenly, from the DJ table, Lizzie flailed her arms at Paloma and shot her a panicked look. Once she had Paloma's attention, Lizzie pointed toward the back of the courtyard. Paloma's eyes zoomed in and caught Mr. Farill dashing off in the direction of the locked storage room, where Gael had just left to set up.

It couldn't be! Paloma felt every hair on her body stand up. Mr. Farill was too early—why was he going back there now? She never got a chance to give Mr. Farill the note. And now Gael would get caught!

Lizzie suddenly started playing her trumpet over a microphone. A crowd including Paloma's mom and Professor

Breton gathered around her as she began to play a sweet melody. All of this was happening too soon.

Paloma followed after Mr. Farill. He ducked through the tree branches, unaware that Paloma was close behind. She hoped Gael had already positioned the cell phone and taken cover.

Mr. Farill paused at the open door and looked down toward the tree where Paloma had discovered the metal box. Paloma stooped low behind some thick branches and watched him. Finally, he stepped into the room. She snuck close to the door and waited, praying under her breath that Gael was safe and hidden away under the desk as they planned.

From inside the room, she heard rustling and scraping sounds. So far, so good. If he had discovered Gael, Mr. Farill would be shouting for security. When she peered inside the room, Tavo's father was pushing back the wheelchair and pulling up the loose tile from the floor. He suddenly moved toward the ladder and grabbed a metal wand with a hook at the end of it. Paloma gazed over to where the desk was covered by a blanket. Gael was under it filming everything.

Mr. Farill moved back to the hole in the floor and dipped the metal hook. He pulled out the velvet pouch as Paloma approached.

"Is everything okay, Mr. Farill?" Paloma asked in the sweetest voice she could muster. "Do you need my help with anything?"

He looked back at her, surprised that she was there. Paloma took a few steps closer.

"Everything is fine. Please go back to Tavo."

"She is with me," said Tavo's voice behind her. "What's going on, Dad? What's this room?"

Paloma stiffened. Why was Tavo here? Mr. Farill didn't seem to know, either. His expression changed from surprised to annoyed, before settling back in a charming smile. Paloma stayed quiet, unsure of what to say next. From beneath the desk, she saw Gael's phone peeking through a rip in the blanket to capture everything. Any moment she knew Lizzie would stop playing her trumpet and start broadcasting everything they were saying to the entire party.

"Nothing is going on, Son. You two should go back up to the celebration. Your mom wanted more cups, so I've come looking for them."

"Cups?" Tavo's eyes dropped toward the velvet pouch he held in his hand.

Lizzie's playing stopped. The audience applauded. Now was the moment for Paloma to expose Mr. Farill as the true thief. But she hadn't expected Tavo to show up, and she wasn't sure how that would affect her plan.

"Mr. Farill, that bag you're holding is so pretty. Is it velvet? What's inside?" Paloma asked, speaking in a slow careful voice and loving the look of annoyance on Mr. Farill's face.

"I'll take that!" roared a voice with a thick Russian accent from behind Tavo and Paloma. It was the Trench

Coat Man. As he limped past her toward Mr. Farill, she felt her stomach drop. Behind the silver mask he wore, she caught his angry glance and trembled. The stocky man she had seen Mr. Farill meeting at the market swaggered in, wearing a black leather coat and red metallic mask. The stocky man closed the door tightly behind him. "What are these children doing here?"

Mr. Farill handed the pouch to the Trench Coat Man.

"You're early," Mr. Farill growled at him. "They're just about to return to the party."

"Dad, what's going on?" Tavo asked, pulling Paloma protectively behind him and looking back and forth from his dad to the Trench Coat Man.

The Trench Coat Man ignored Tavo and said something in Russian to Mr. Farill.

"Why don't you two return to your friends?" Mr. Farill said. "These are business associates." He smiled at Tavo. "Don't worry, Son."

"Let's go, Paloma," Tavo said, but Paloma sealed her feet to the ground. The plan was to get Mr. Farill to confess to his crimes over the speaker Lizzie had set up. Tavo's arrival and the presence of the Trench Coat Man and his friend had not been in the plan, but she couldn't give up now. Her heart raced as she tried to figure out what to do next.

"I really want to see what's in that pouch. I mean, you pulled it from that hole in the ground. Didn't you, Mr. Farill? What is it?"

Mr. Farill's smile tightened into a toothy snarl. "I'm losing my patience with you, Paloma."

"C'mon, Paloma. He's being a jerk. Let's just go," Tavo said again, tugging at her arm.

She pulled away from Tavo and stepped closer to the Trench Coat Man. "Do you recognize me?" she said with a forced smile. The Trench Coat Man grinned and rubbed his chin where she had kicked him the night he'd grabbed her from under the desk.

"What are you talking about?" Tavo asked her. "What's going on?"

"You should show us what's inside the pouch," she said. The Trench Coat Man let out a small chuckle. The stocky man next to him laughed, showing a set of gold teeth. Paloma gave a side glance to where Gael was still recording everything.

"If you insist," the Trench Coat Man said.

"Is this really necessary?" Mr. Farill asked as the Trench Coat Man opened the small box.

The Trench Coat Man's face went white. "What's the meaning of this?" he bellowed, turning the box to face Mr. Farill. Inside was Mr. Farill's gold cuff link. Paloma smirked.

"Is that your cuff link?" Tavo asked. "What's going on? Why—"

"Where's the ring?" the Trench Coat Man growled, and lurched for Mr. Farill's tuxedo collar. "You better not be messing with me!" he threatened. "We made a deal! Our buyer isn't going to be happy!"

"It was there!" Mr. Farill cried. "I hid it here in the hole. I just checked on it last week—it was there!"

Tavo jumped in and tried to pull the man off his father. But the Trench Coat Man pushed Tavo back, slamming him into Paloma, who let out a weak wail.

Suddenly, Gael leapt out from under the desk. "Leave her alone!"

The short, stocky man grabbed Gael in a headlock. Every hair on Paloma's body stood up as Gael grimaced in pain.

"Let him go!" she screamed.

The Trench Coat Man gave his friend a nod. Soon, Gael was out of the headlock, but his arms were pulled behind his back.

"Who do we have here?" Mr. Farill asked. Paloma narrowed her eyes at Gael, warning him against making his speech, but he stood up as straight as he could and locked eyes with Mr. Farill.

"My name is Gael Lorca Castillo. Son of Antonio Manuel Castillo," he said. "You framed my father. Now you will confess like the scum you are."

"Gael Castillo?" Tavo repeated. "Your Spanish tutor?"

Paloma bit down on her lower lip. She was scared for Gael. Who knew what Mr. Farill would do next!

"Your father was a fool!" Mr. Farill spat. "I gave him the

choice to get a cut of what I was selling the ring for, but he lacked vision. He believed Frida's artwork should stay in Mexico. He was a fool, and you're a fool for thinking you could take the ring from me. Now hand it over! I know you have it."

Gael gulped hard and started muttering in Spanish as he patted his pants, pretending he was looking for the ring. Paloma clutched her purse straps. The ring was tucked inside.

"What are you saying, Dad?" Tavo said. "Why are you acting like this?"

"Your father is smuggling Frida's peacock ring out of Mexico," Paloma said. Her heart thumped hard in her chest. Poor Tavo. She regretted him being with them, but there was no hiding the truth now. Mr. Farill didn't love art. He loved money. His mask was off. She hoped Lizzie and the entire party was hearing everything. "He sells the artifacts he steals. He framed Antonio Castillo for it—"

"Be quiet, you conniving brat!" Mr. Farill snarled.

"You've really lost it, Dad," Tavo said, shaking his head.

"Me? These *traviesos* have been running around together behind your back and trading notes. They're the ones who broke into our home. Sergei here has been watching them since you told me that Paloma's tutor was Gael Castillo." Mr. Farill gestured toward the stocky man who stood behind Gael. Gael and Paloma exchanged a quick, confused look. They thought Sergei was the Trench Coat Man's name. "I knew then that the Castillos were up to something." Mr. Farill turned from Tavo to Gael. "Now you and your sister can join your dad in jail."

"You belong in jail!" Gael hollered.

"That's enough!" the Trench Coat Man growled. He tapped his chest. "We have what we need."

Mr. Farill gave the Trench Coat Man a startled look. "What are you talking about?"

A chill went up Paloma's spine as the door burst open behind them. A bright light pointed at Mr. Farill. The blood drained from his face, and he raised his hands up over his head.

"Step away from the children!" a loud booming voice called from the door. Paloma knew that woman's voice. She spun around to see the Fortune-Teller holding a gun . . . and a badge.

Chapter 27

The Troublemakers

Behind the Fortune-Teller, a group of police officers dressed in black uniforms swarmed into the room. She quickly handcuffed Sergei, while the Trench Coat Man handcuffed Mr. Farill, then shoved him toward another police officer to lead him out of the room.

"Dad!" Tavo cried out. "What's going on?"

"Don't worry, son!" he yelled over his shoulder. "I've been set up. Tell your mom to call my lawyer . . ."

Paloma glanced over at Tavo. His face flushed red as if he'd just been smacked. A police officer moved to guide him toward the door, but he raised his hands to stop her.

"I'm fine," he said softly, and walked out of the room alone.

Paloma remained frozen, waiting for answers from the Trench Coat Man and the Fortune-Teller.

"Who are you?" she asked them. Gael stood next to her, clearly too shocked to speak.

"We're Interpol officers. International police," the Fortune-Teller answered. "We've been tracking art smuggling between Mexico and Russia for a while now. Without your help, we couldn't have caught Sergei or Mr. Farill."

"And Mr. Castillo?" Paloma asked. "Can you get him out of jail now?"

The Trench Coat Man nodded and smiled. "He'll be home by daybreak. Do you have a certain piece of evidence for us?"

"What?" Paloma asked. Gael nudged her. "Oh yeah, the ring. I almost forgot." She chuckled, pulled the peacock ring from her bag, and handed it to the Fortune-Teller.

"Nice touch with the cuff link," the Trench Coat Man said with a wink. "I never saw that coming."

"Thanks," Paloma said.

The Fortune-Teller looked over the peacock ring. "It's beautiful. No wonder you asked me for one," she teased. "Good job, kids."

One of the police officers threw a blanket around Gael and started to walk him out of the room. Gael looked back and called for Paloma.

"I'm not leaving without her," he said. Before she knew it, the Trench Coat Man had taken off his namesake coat and covered her shoulders with it. She clasped Gael's hand as they walked out of the room together.

"Mr. Farill called us *traviesos*," Paloma said. "What does that mean?"

"It means 'troublemakers.'" Gael smiled and shrugged. "Maybe we are?"

Paloma let out a deep breath. "Definitely."

Once outside in the courtyard, Lizzie came running up to Gael and Paloma and hugged them.

"We did it!" she squealed.

All the guests whispered and mumbled back and forth to one another as Mr. Farill and the man named Sergei were escorted through the courtyard and into flashing police cars.

Paloma's mom rushed to her, clutched her tight, and kissed her head. "Are you okay?" she asked, pressing Paloma's face between her hands. "Are you hurt?"

"I'm fine," Paloma said.

Tavo ran to his mother. For a moment, he held Paloma's gaze, but then he pulled his mask off and looked down at the floor. She had never meant to hurt him. She tried to lock eyes with him again, but his mom pulled him away toward the exit. He never looked back. Paloma felt a lump form in her throat as she wondered if that was the last time she'd see him.

"*Damas y caballeros,*" the Fortune-Teller announced into the microphone to gather the guests. She went on to explain that they were Interpol officers and, although they apologized for the interruption to the party, they had no choice but to take action in order to protect the three young heroes who secured one of Frida Kahlo's most treasured pieces of jewelry. Gael translated for Paloma everything the Fortune-Teller said. Guests muttered back and forth to one another and stole glances at Paloma, Gael, and Lizzie, who huddled close together.

"Because of the bravery of these children tonight on Frida Kahlo's birthday," Gael translated, "the peacock ring that was stolen from Frida Kahlo, Casa Azul, and the people of Mexico has been returned safely."

The Fortune-Teller held the peacock ring up for everyone to see. Excited squeals filled the night air as rays of sparkling blue and green light reflected around the courtyard. Everyone cheered, and Paloma finally found herself able to smile as police officers patted her back and people from the crowd blew kisses to the three children.

"That was some party," Professor Breton said, giving Paloma a high five.

Paloma pouted. "I feel a little bad about it."

"Why?"

"We had to ruin Frida's party to get her peacock ring back," Paloma said.

"Ruin her party? Have you learned nothing about the artist?" Professor Breton said, shaking his head. "I think this is exactly the kind of party Frida would have loved. International police? Russian smugglers? A fortune-teller who arrests everyone? She would have been thrilled."

Paloma nodded. He was right. She gazed up toward Frida's bedroom, where her urn was set atop a table.

"Feliz cumpleaños, Frida," Paloma said softly.

Chapter 28

The Lost Boy

As soon she arrived at Casa Azul for the award ceremony, everyone started taking pictures of Paloma and her mom. Several people gave her flowers and called her *la Palomita Valiente*. The brave little dove. The newspaper even ran a story with that headline detailing how Paloma, Gael, and Lizzie had confronted a Russian jewelry smuggler and the wealthy and powerful Mr. Farill, and returned Frida's missing jewelry to Casa Azul.

Paloma enjoyed the attention and looked forward to receiving a medal from the mayor, but mostly she wanted to see Gael and Lizzie, the Fortune-Teller, and the Trench Coat Man one more time before she returned home to Kansas.

The Trench Coat Man's real name was Mikhail Alexeev.

From newspaper articles, Paloma learned how Mikhail and Rosa Zuniga, fortune-teller/Interpol officer, had been tracking art that was being smuggled between Mexico and Russia. For a year, Mikhail had spent time infiltrating underground operations, when he received a message from a man named Sergei Rykov who was helping an unknown client sell a valuable artifact designed by the popular artist Frida Kahlo. Mikhail quickly called his fellow officer Rosa Zuniga to help him with the case because he believed an innocent man was in jail for stealing the artifact from Casa Azul. So Mikhail quickly disguised himself as a Russian smuggler and made contact with Sergei, who then put him in touch with Mr. Farill. Tavo's father had been so anxious to sell Frida's peacock ring—which was worth over five million dollars—that he became sloppy when he framed Mr. Castillo. None of the museum staff believed Mr. Castillo could do such a thing. Suspecting something strange was going on, they quickly began to install security cameras all over Casa Azul.

While Mikhail was waiting for the right moment to capture Mr. Farill and Sergei, Rosa was charged with watching Mr. Castillo's children. They knew that Gael and Lizzie were actively trying to free their father and needed extra protection. Rosa disguised herself as a fortune-teller to keep an eye on them. But Interpol couldn't figure out how Paloma was involved.

Paloma remembered how the Trench Coat Man had given her a look of confusion when he saw her under the desk. Now she knew it was because he was expecting Gael or Lizzie. According to the newspapers, Mikhail and Rosa were blindsided when the twelve-year-old American showed up asking about a peacock ring and hanging out at Casa Azul. They praised Paloma for her bravery and smarts in finding the ring and setting into motion a plan to get a confession from Mr. Farill that would set Antonio Castillo free. Rosa even called her a "future Interpol detective." And now she and her friends were being honored by the city!

As Paloma entered the courtyard, Gael and Lizzie rushed up to her with their dad close behind them.

Mr. Castillo gave Paloma a big hug.

"I still can't thank you enough," he said. "You are part of our family now."

Paloma nodded. She felt like she might cry. This, for her, was the true reward of the day. She didn't need anything else.

A mariachi band started to play, marking the beginning of the ceremony. As the mayor introduced Rosa Zuniga to present a medal and check for five thousand dollars to each of the kids, Paloma glanced to the side of the courtyard and noticed a boy with brownish hair staring into the fountain. He wore a light blue polo shirt and beige pants, and looked very familiar. "Tavo," Paloma whispered. When she looked again, she caught a better glimpse of the boy's face. Her heart sank. It wasn't Tavo.

She'd tried calling him the day after the masquerade

party, but he hadn't answered. She didn't blame him. Since the party, news of his father's crimes was in every local newspaper. For all she knew, Tavo wasn't even in Coyoacán anymore. Today she was hoping to learn more about what was happening to his family from Rosa or Mikhail. She didn't feel right returning to Kansas without knowing if he was okay.

After the ceremony, Paloma, Gael, and Lizzie sat at a long craft table with the other kids in the audience. To celebrate Frida's legacy, they would create their own self-portraits. Some press hovered around them and took pictures as they painted. Paloma was just about to throw her first attempt away and start a new portrait when suddenly Rosa and Mikhail took a seat next to her.

"I have an update for you, *traviesos*," Rosa said. "It's not great news, I'm afraid." Paloma braced herself for news about Tavo. "The Farills are going back to Spain tomorrow. As part of the deal they've made, Mr. Farill won't go to jail, but he will no longer be welcome in Mexico. They will be forced to sell their house and all their property here."

The news stung Paloma. No jail time for Mr. Farill. Gael and Lizzie fell strangely silent.

"A deal? Even though Mr. Castillo had to suffer in jail for so long?" she asked.

"Sorry we couldn't do more," Rosa finally said.

"We're very sorry," Mikhail added.

"No, it's okay. At least our dad is free," Lizzie spoke up. "That's all that matters now." She put an arm around Gael's shoulders and gave him a kiss on the cheek.

Rosa pulled an envelope out of her purse. "As for Tavo Farill . . . he asked me to give this to you, Paloma. It's open because we had to read it to ensure that he wasn't trying to threaten or intimidate you."

Paloma stared down at the opened envelope. "I understand."

Gael and Lizzie stood. "Rosita, have you ever tried a mango-*chile paleta*?" Gael asked. "It's sweet and spicy like us." Lizzie groaned at the same old joke her brother always made.

Rosa got up, patting Paloma one last time on her shoulder, but Mikhail remained.

"Paloma, I've been thinking about what I'd tell my own daughter in this situation," he started. Paloma smiled. Only a few days ago, she was afraid of the Trench Coat Man. Now she admired him and knew she could trust whatever he said. "I know it must have seemed like I was the bad guy. But it was just a disguise. And no matter how you feel about the Farill boy, you were never the bad guy in this entire ordeal. You were brave, smart, and when it counted, you did the right thing. You shouldn't feel guilty for anything." Mikhail gave her a gentle smile. "I just wanted you to know that before you read that letter, *Palomita Valiente*."

Paloma looked down at the letter. "Thank you," she said. Mikhail left and joined the others for a *paleta*. Paloma was grateful for the privacy. She opened Tavo's letter.

Dear Paloma,

By the time you get this note, I will probably already be back in Spain with my family. I wanted you to know that after reading everything in the papers about my dad's part in framing Mr. Castillo, I don't blame you for helping your friends. I admire you for it. Please tell the Castillos that I'm happy their dad is free. I regret what my dad did to their family more than I can say.

My mom and I are returning to her family home in Barcelona. My dad is not invited to go with us. I think my mom is finally done with him. It's weird, but it doesn't bother me. Right now, I'm just going to take care of my mom. She needs me.

I hope you enjoy the rest of your time in Coyoacán and have safe travels back to Kansas. Whenever I think about us never seeing each other again, I think about that song that played the first time we met. Do you remember? "El niño perdido"? The lost boy. In the end, the trumpets find each other and they play together side by side. That's how I think it will be for you and me. Someday, somewhere, we

will hear each other's voices, and like those trumpets
we will come together as long-lost friends. That is my hope.

Your friend always,

Tavo

Chapter 29

Finders of Lost Things

The night before Paloma and her mom were to catch their flight back to Kansas, Paloma couldn't sleep. Even though the clock said it was eleven thirty, Paloma sat up in bed, switched on the lamp on her nightstand, and grabbed her memory box. She scattered all the note cards onto her blanket and began to read them one by one. The ones that held memories of her father were now mixed in with new memories she had made with Gael and Lizzie. For so long, Paloma had yearned for her own memories of her father, but she'd discovered something better. Even though her father wasn't with her in Mexico, he was with her every step of the way. She had arrived in Mexico as his little bird, but now she was leaving as *Palomita Valiente*.

"*Gracias*, Papá," she said. "For giving me my own memories."

Her chest heaved as tears came to her eyes. That's when she heard a guitar thrumming and the soft melody of a silver trumpet outside. She rushed to her window. A few seconds later, her mom dashed in.

"It's a *serenata*!" her mom squealed, taking her seat at the windowsill.

Paloma shook her head, giggling, and went to sit on her mom's lap. Her mom sang along with Gael and Lizzie. Paloma bobbed her head to the upbeat song. Once they were done, Gael rolled out a large sheet of paper.

"Paloma . . ." Gael shouted from below. "You are our best friend now, and we made this painting for you so you'll never forget us." Lizzie took the painting and held it up in front of her. In the painting, Gael and Lizzie sat side by side holding hands. Behind them, a large peacock spread its wings. "It says . . ." Gael continued.

"For Paloma, we searched for a peacock and found a beautiful dove. We'll never forget you. With all our love, your friends forever, Gael and Lizzie."

Paloma's mom wiped her eyes.

Paloma swallowed the knot forming in her throat. "I made a self-portrait for you, too," she shouted down. "But it's horrible. I can't paint at all." Gael and Lizzie laughed at her. "You want to see it?"

"Yes!" they screamed up at her.

"Let's go!" her mom gushed.

Paloma slipped on her flip-flops and grabbed the self-portrait she had started at Casa Azul. In the painting, Paloma had her hair loose around her face. Around her neck she had painted the red opal necklace and the Aztec eagle soldier medallion. The background was filled with green-and-turquoise peacock feathers, Frida's blue house, Lizzie's silver trumpet, Gael's black knit hat, and lots of blue sky. In her hands, she held the delicate peacock ring.

The three mystery solvers and finders of lost things gathered, laughed, and joked. Paloma's mom didn't mind one bit that they wanted to drink hot chocolate, eat churros, and stay up all night. Somewhere between midnight and six in the morning, when Paloma had to leave for the airport with her mom, the kids added three note cards to the bottom of Paloma's self-portrait:

Viva Frida!

Viva friendship!

Viva memories!

Author's Note

On one of my first ever visits to New York City, I went to the Museum of Modern Art (aka: MOMA) in midtown Manhattan. Ever since I was a child I had heard about this amazing museum and I was anxious to visit and see paintings by Jackson Pollack, Andy Warhol, Pablo Picasso, and Vincent van Gogh. As I stood at the entrance, studying a brochure that mapped on which floor I could find Van Gogh, I overheard a museum staff member telling another tourist that there was a Frida Kahlo self-portrait on the fifth floor. My heart was on fire! I had been a young girl when I was first exposed to the artwork of Frida Kahlo. One of her self-portraits was in a book at our house and I immediately connected with Frida's face and loved the flowers in her hair. Even at a young age, I felt like Frida was trying to tell me something about self-identity and about standing strong against poverty, bullying, and all of the obstacles I was facing at the time. Forget the map! I bolted up the escalators and sped past the many paintings by Picasso to find Frida.

Once I reached the gallery where Frida was supposed to be, three tween girls stepped in front of me and found Frida's self-portrait, *Fulang-Chang and I*, before I did. I hung back and watched them as the girls locked into a long silent gaze with Frida. After a few seconds of silence, one of the girls exclaimed, "Call the salon! She needs a serious brow wax." Their first reaction left me both amused and inspired, and it spurred this mystery novel. I ended up using that line, "Call the salon!" for Paloma's initial reaction to seeing a Frida Kahlo self-portrait.

Me, Frida, and the Secret of the Peacock Ring is a fictional novel featuring the very real artwork and life of the artist Frida Kahlo. I've taken creative license with some of the details in the story, especially in regard to the missing peacock ring. Here is the truth: The idea for the missing peacock ring came from reading the book *Frida: A Biography of Frida Kahlo* by Hayden Herrera. In the biography, the author relates that Frida had told a close friend that she wanted to have a peacock ring. Frida even went so far as to collect "little stones" and sketch a picture of it. Since I also love peacocks and I like jewelry (too much!), I was fascinated by this peacock ring and began to search for it on Frida's fingers in every photograph I came across. I never found it on her fingers and I wondered what happened. Did she ever get her ring? Where is it now?

And there I found my story.

It was on a visit to Frida's home, known as La Casa Azul, in Coyoacán that my story truly developed. At La Casa Azul, I learned that after Frida died, her husband, Diego Rivera, put many pieces of her wardrobe (including jewelry, clothes, and accessories) into a bathroom near her studio and locked it up. Shortly before Rivera died in 1957, he asked a close friend, Dolores Olmedo, to keep the room locked for an additional fifteen years. Dolores Olmedo ended up keeping the room locked until her own death in 2002. Now, with the bathroom unlocked, many of Frida's personal items are on display in a special exhibit at La Casa Azul. Adding the true story about the locked bathroom holding some of Frida's most cherished jewelry, including a pair of earrings Pablo Picasso had given her, was just what my novel needed and gave my invented tale about the peacock ring a bit more mystery.

In the novel, Paloma is described as "obsessed" with a book series featuring her all-time favorite detective, Lulu Pennywhistle. Lulu sprung from my imagination, but I named her after my friend Lulu Carvajal. There are also a few character names in the book that are taken from real people in Frida's life. The family name Farill, used for Tavo and his parents, belonged to Frida's long-time doctor and confidant, Dr. Juan Farill, who Frida actually credited with saving her life during some of her darkest moments. In reality, Dr. Farill was nothing like Mr. Farill in my novel. The real Dr. Farill adored Frida and, in return, Frida deeply cherished his friendship and even painted a self-portrait with the doctor to show her gratitude to him.

Throughout the novel, I describe several of Frida's paintings as best as I can. These interpretations of her paintings are my own as seen through the eyes of my young protagonist Paloma Marquez. These interpretations should not be considered the only interpretations. For when it comes to the artwork of Frida Kahlo, there are many opinions and many contrasting interpretations, and I don't think any of them are wrong.

Finally, because I grew up exposed to Frida Kahlo's artwork from a very young age, I wanted to make sure I handled her with the admiration I feel in my heart for her. If you'd like to read more about Frida or see her artwork, I recommend Hayden Herrera's book *Frida: A Biography of Frida Kahlo*. It was an indispensible resource to me while writing this novel. Additionally, I also highly recommend visiting Frida Kahlo's museum, La Casa Azul, located in beautiful Coyoacán, Mexico. It is definitely worth the trip. And maybe I'll see you there!

Acknowledgments

With gratitude to the following people:

First, my editor, Anna Bloom, for her warmth and guidance as I completed this novel; Abigail McAden, who stepped in and assisted when a certain adorable baby came onto the scene. And to the rest of the Scholastic team for their enthusiasm and professional support: Monica Palenzuela, Nina Goffi, Michelle Campbell, Lizette Serrano, and the amazing Robin Hoffman and her school market squad.

Rafael López, for lending his talents to make the cover a true piece of art. Nancy Villafranca, for her knowledge and expertise.

Jane True, Victoria Dixon, and Lisa Cindrich for their helpful feedback during early versions of the manuscript. My young editors: Ava, Kori, Eden, Ana, Lydia, and Taylor for their honesty. Brook Nasseri for being a wonderful intern. Veronica Romo for her thoughtful review of my Spanish.

For the unstoppable team at Full Circle Literary Agency, especially my agent, Adriana Dominguez Ferrari.

Mis alumnos at CEDI in Guadalajara: My memories of their heart, humor, and pride in Mexico carried me through this novel.

My family, for their love and patience.

About the Author

Angela Cervantes is the author of the middle grade novels *Gaby, Lost and Found* and *Allie, First At Last*. Angela is a daughter of a retired middle school teacher who instilled in her a love for reading and storytelling. Angela writes from her home in Kansas. When she is not writing, Angela enjoys reading, running, gazing up at clouds, and taking advantage of Taco Tuesdays everywhere she goes. Learn more about Angela Cervantes at www.angelacervantes.com.

Author photo by Kenny Johnson